"Each bird we meet in these chapters comes to life, reminding us again of the Creator's mercy for all of His creation. Kehler's practical knowledge and care for winged creatures create a desire to look and listen more carefully to the common and extraordinary birds in our neighborhoods. This book is a charming gift to introduce birders to the One who protects us all under His wings."

— Elizabeth Hoekstra
 Founder of Sweetwater Ministries, author, and speaker

"While I do not consider myself a bird lover, I do consider the outdoors to be God's sanctuary—where God can change my perspective (Psalm 73:17). I love to garden in the sun, Rollerblade along the river, and lounge in my hammock beneath the trees. There in His sancturary, I often see birds. After reading *Wings of Mercy*, the birds themselves will be more than spot color in the scenery. . . . *Wings of Mercy* is perfect inspirational reading for anyone who enjoys nature — bird lover, or not."

— Marita Littauer
 Speaker/Author, President, CLASServices, Inc.

LAURIE KEHLER

WINGS *of* MERCY

Shelter under His wings!
Laurie

BETHANYHOUSE
MINNEAPOLIS, MINNESOTA

Published by Bethany House Publishers
11400 Hampshire Avenue South
Bloomington, Minnesota 55438
www.bethanyhouse.com

Bethany House Publishers is a Division of
Baker Book House Company, Grand Rapids, Michigan.

Printed in the United States of America

Library of Congress Cataloging-in-Publication Data

Kehler, Laurie Ostby.
   Wings of mercy : spiritual reflections from the birds of the air / by Laurie Ostby
Kehler.
     p. cm.
   ISBN 0-7642-2693-2 (pbk.)
   1. Bird watchers—Religious life. 2. Bird watching—Religious aspects—
Christianity. 3. Christian women—Religious life. 4. Christian life. I. Title.

   BV4596.B57K44   2003
   242'.68—dc21
                                                2003000977

～ Dedication ～

For Tom

Your steadfast love and support

enable me to soar.

~ Acknowledgments ~

I am indebted to my critique group, who
spent countless Monday afternoons
pouring over this manuscript:
Cathy Armstrong, Barbara Milligan,
Pat Sikora, and Judy Squier.

Thanks to the talented Steve Laube,
who believed in the growing popularity of birding
and helped this project take flight.

And also to the patient
and eagle-eyed editing of Julie Smith.

And finally, thank you to my mother, who
first taught me the wonder and delight
of recognizing the different songbird calls.

⟶ *About the Author* ⟶

Laurie Kehler is the author of *Gardening Mercies — Finding God in Your Garden* and *How Do I Love Thee — Conversation Starters for a Romantic Evening*. She and her husband, Tom, live in the San Francisco Bay area, where she is a casual but enthusiastic birder. Her favorite bird is the brilliant cardinal — no wait, the brave little chickadee — er, maybe the winsome meadowlark. . . .

For more information regarding speaking engagements and additional materials, you can e-mail her at:

Email: LK@LaurieKehler.com

Snail mail: PO Box 3194, Half Moon Bay, CA 94019

For other books and products, visit the website at:

https://www.LaurieKehler.com

To book Laurie to speak, visit: LaurieKehler.com/speaking

~ Contents ~

～ Bluebird ～

It took us twenty-five white-knuckled minutes to reach the property at the top of the mountain. Our real-estate agent kept turning around to talk with us while she negotiated hairpin turns with heart-stopping drop-offs. After we crossed a stream, gunned vertical climbs that made San Francisco look like a bunny hill, and survived axle-twisting ruts and bumps, I was just thankful to have made it alive, never mind the fantastic scenery. But what distracted my stomach from turning itself inside out upon our arrival was the cheery bluebird that flew straight to our car and perched itself on our side mirror. While my husband sucked in his breath at the view of the Pacific Ocean, my head was turned to watch our cute welcoming agent.

A bluebird! I thought, definitely a wonderful omen for this

property. I hadn't seen any bluebirds
growing up in Wisconsin (not that I was
looking for them) and was utterly
charmed by this visitation. He
cocked his head, looked around,
sang to us a little, and gazed at himself in
our rearview mirrors. While the real-estate agent
waxed on about the property and its benefits, I stood trans-
fixed by our blue-feathered visitor with his plump red breast.
Despite the fact that he left copious amounts of digestive evidence on the car by the time he fluttered off, I was thrilled
that the proverbial bluebird of happiness came with the
property. (And yes, we did buy it.)

Later, when I remarked about our unique feathered visitor to our neighbor Peter, he said, "Oh, well, of course, the
reason we have so many bluebirds up here is because of the
bluebird trail we set up." *Bluebird trail?* I had never heard of
this.

According to Donald and Lillian Stokes (they have a fantastic Web site[1] and have authored many books on birding),
the first bluebird trail was created by Thomas E. Musselman
when he placed birdhouses along stretches of a road. In the
1920s and 1930s he could see the native bluebird was getting
crowded out of prime nesting areas by the imported European house sparrows and starlings. So in 1934, Musselman

---

[1] *www.stokesbooks.com.*

started a "bluebird trail." Eventually, he had a trail of more than one thousand boxes in Adams County, Illinois. Around the same time, William Duncan set up bluebird trails in Jefferson County, Kentucky, and also created a great basic bluebird nest box. These two efforts were the beginning of bluebird conservation. Thanks to hundreds of Americans across the country who are putting up bluebird trails and making their backyards a haven for them, bluebirds are slowly growing from sparse populations to more abundant ones.

You can learn more about how to create and maintain a bluebird trail by reading the Stokes's book *The Bluebird Book: The Complete Guide to Attracting Bluebirds*, or by visiting the National Bluebird Society Web site, *www.nabluebirdsociety.org*.

However, you don't need a bluebird trail to encourage the bluebird of happiness to come to your backyard; just provide the right environment. In the summer, bluebirds need bluebird houses (these have specific measurements to deter other birds and predators; see the Stokes's book), a lot of insects, and low vegetation so they can find those insects. Therefore, blasting your yard with chemicals to kill all bugs will ensure you have no bluebirds. They hunt for these insects from perches, so make sure you have some bushes, chairs, or other areas where they can perch. Bluebirds also enjoy berry-producing trees, shrubs, and vines. Your local nursery will know what grows best in your area. In the winter, these berry-producing plants are vital to their survival as they provide shelter as well.

Not only do bluebirds enjoy insects and berries, but they also love mealy worms. When I was in Madison, Wisconsin, my mother and I were visiting this wonderful birding store on University Avenue called Chickadee Depot. A young woman walked in and ordered lots of mealy worms. "What do you feed with those?" I asked her. "Bluebirds," she sighed. "They practically go through a box a day, but how can you say no to *bluebirds*?"

Why do we work so hard to create conditions for the bluebird to grace our yards? What is it about this charming little bird that warms our heart, thrills us when we see it, and imparts this charming affiliation with happiness?

Bluebirds have long been associated with good luck and happiness. Henry David Thoreau said, "The bluebird carries the sky on his back." Many greeting cards start out with, "May the bluebird of happiness . . ." In the movie *The Wizard of Oz*, Dorothy sings about a better place she'd like to escape to—over the rainbow where dreams come true—a place where bluebirds fly.

We've all felt like that at times. When the economy is stumbling, my husband doesn't know if he can keep up with the demands at work, and my hopes and dreams never seem to materialize, I too would like to fly over the rainbow to a happier, saner place. Whether it's over the rainbow or over the next fence, we are convinced it's better anywhere but here. My friends' lives all look simpler and happier to me; their homes are cleaner and their bodies are trimmer. I frequently have to remind myself to not swallow the lie that they are happier than I am. That may or may not be true, but it's probably not due to what they possess compared to what I lack.

Happiness is big business in America. Indeed, we think it is our God-given right. The Declaration of Independence pronounces that our mission statement as a country is, ". . . life, liberty and the pursuit of happiness." Popular speaker Tony Campolo states that while most Japanese parents would say they want their children to be successful, most Americans, when asked what they want for their children, will sigh and say, "I just want them to be *happy*."

Most of us would like to be happy all the time, and we will go to great lengths to ensure that the bluebird of happiness sits on our shoulder. We change our spouses or jobs or homes. We get our thighs sucked, tummies tucked, and faces lifted. We "shop till we drop," overindulge at the table, and fill our glasses too many times. How do I know this?

Because I am guilty of some of these (and others I frequently consider).

Our TV shows, movies, and books convey the message that if we marry the right person, if we get the right job, if our children would do the right thing, if we could move to a bigger home, lose that weight, we would *find* happiness. It's ironic to me we're all chasing this land of never-never, this Atlantis called Happiness. I find it ironic because we are living in the world's most prosperous nation, yet the whole culture is set up that in order to maintain the economy people need to keep buying things. We are fed the lie from TV, magazines, and radio that we don't possess enough talent, we aren't attractive enough, and we don't have enough stuff. I know this because I used to work in advertising and every ad campaign we thought of started out with creating the perception of a need (that only our product could fill). Like gerbils on the exercise wheel, we can never reach this destination or fill this Grand Canyon of need.

I saved a greeting card I bought years ago. I never gave it to anyone because I felt the message was for me. Me, who constantly compared what I had to what others had and always found myself lacking. It was a quotation from Abraham Lincoln: "Most people are as happy as they make up their minds to be."

I like this quotation because it points out that the state of happiness isn't something we run after, hoping it descends on us. It's a state of mind we *choose*. We can choose to be content with what we have and who we are.

Research backs up this idea. According to *The Journal of Happiness Studies*, edited by sociology professor Ruut Veenhoven of Erasmus University, Rotterdam, in the Netherlands, the single most important factor in someone's state of happiness is close ties to friends and family. Wealth did not matter as much as this factor. Climate or country did not matter as much either.

Establishing close ties with friends and family doesn't just happen. It takes work. It's a choice. Ask anyone on the third day of Thanksgiving vacation. It's amazing how easily family members can hit your hot buttons and annoy you with unerring accuracy. My mother made a humorous needlepoint pillow that resides in her guest room asking, "You *are* leaving by Sunday, aren't you?"

Marriage seminars point out that love is, most of the time, not a feeling but a choice. I don't always feel ooeygooey toward my husband. Sometimes in the middle of a disagreement we don't even like each other much, but we are committed to loving each other. People often ask us, "How did you find each other? You have such a good marriage!" They have the erroneous belief that there is a lot of love in our marriage because we just happened to have found the right person. I don't think it's because we found the right person; it's because we are willing to make the right *choices*. Choices to drop our pride and say, "I'm sorry, I was wrong, you were right." Choices to put the other person first and do what *he* wants to do this Saturday. Choices to not compare our spouse unfavorably with another's spouse.

Wise King Solomon also talked about happiness, or contentment, as being the product of right choices. In the book of Ecclesiastes he says, "To enjoy your work and to accept your lot in life—that is indeed a gift from God. The person who does that will not need to look back with sorrow on his past, for God gives him joy" (Ecclesiastes 5:20 TLB). This concept is stated again in 1 Timothy 6:6–8, "But godliness with contentment is great gain. For we brought nothing into the world, and we can take nothing out of it. But if we have food and clothing, we will be content with that." This is the opposite message we are getting from the world around us, which is, *What we don't have will make us happy—go for it—just do it.* The Scriptures are telling us that happiness is choosing to enjoy what we have and being thankful for it.

Author Anne Lamott talks about a friend of hers named Paul. He's in his eighties and has the right outlook on life. He says, "I try to enjoy life the way it is, because that's the way it's going to be anyway." How different this approach is from my usual response of anger and power struggles to try to change things to my liking.

I easily fall into the trap of thinking, *It's not fair I don't have things when other, less responsible, women do.* My girl friend struggles with thinking, *It's not fair others have a home when we are stuck in a tiny apartment. We would use it for serving others!* Since we both struggle with this comparison problem,

I posted the following words in my bath-room where I'd see them often. It's the recipe for contentment from a mission-ary who knew hard times. These words help me from lapsing into that mistaken state of entitlement, *I should have this, it's my right, everyone else does,* and points my chooser in the right direction.

> Never allow yourself to complain about anything—not even the weather.
> Never picture yourself in any other circumstances or any-where else.
> Never compare your lot with another's.
> Never allow yourself to wish this or that had been other-wise.
> Never dwell on tomorrow—remember that tomorrow is God's, not ours.
>
> E. B. Pusey

I'll admit that sometimes I think these words are impos-sible to follow and a little extreme. But I notice on days when I'm counting my blessings, enjoying the gifts of friend-ship, good health, and loving others, I'm *happy*. It's not a result of anything I purchased or achieved or a place I trav-eled to, it's the result of right choices.

Soon, I'm going to my local wild bird store to buy some bluebird boxes. This, combined with the fruit-bearing shrubs

I intend to plant, will create the conditions to encourage bluebirds to visit my home. When visitors sigh and say, "Oh, how lucky you are! You have the bluebird of happiness visiting your home!" I'll say, "Luck has nothing to do with it. I chose to have them, and so can you."

~ Crows & Ravens ~

Is it just me, or are crows and ravens laying claim to our tranquil neighborhoods? More and more their rough, scratchy *caws* are seemingly everywhere. I always look forward to visiting my parents in the Midwest. I anticipate seeing the cardinal, blue jay, redheaded woodpecker, and other birds from my youth that we don't see in the West. But lately, when I arrive, I don't see many of my favorite songbirds. I do see, however, many more crows and ravens—they seem to be taking over. Their raspy, annoying *caw caw* sounds drown out all the delightful songbirds that might be in the neighborhood.

Apparently, I'm not the only one who is noticing this. I did a search on the Internet and found these comments: "There's been an increase of crows all over the city and they've driven away all the songbirds from the neighborhood. I never see a robin anymore." And, "Over the last few years, a rather large population of crows has come to inhabit my neighborhood and it seems to be on the increase."

I asked my bird-loving friend Janet if she noticed this trend too. "Yes!" she said. "And did you know that a group of crows is called a *murder* of crows?" I looked it up and would add that a group of ravens is referred to as an *unkindness* of ravens. Alfred Hitchcock knew what he was doing when he exploited our distaste by using them in his movie *The Birds*.

My mother (ever the Pollyanna) says these birds perform a valuable function: cleaning up roadkill. I don't know about your neighborhood, but the daily parade of children in strollers and kids on bikes isn't exactly leaving behind a smorgasbord of roadkill in my suburban area. So why have they moved in?

First of all, crows and ravens are smart. A part of the *Corvus* group (which includes jays, nutcrackers, and magpies), they are the smartest of all the bird families. In some psychological tests, crows have performed as well as monkeys.[1] Crows have been known to count to seven, use tools to open things, and associate symbols with events the way humans do.

Ravens (which at twenty-seven inches are bigger than

---

[1] David Sibley, *The Sibley Guide to Bird Life & Behavior* (New York: Alfred A. Knopf, 2001), 412.

crows) have demonstrated uncanny insight into solving problems. Ravens faced with a novel task, such as getting food that is dangling on the end of a string, were able to assess the problem and then use their feet to hold the string and pull the food up. They performed this action without missteps the first time they attempted it.[2]

They are also opportunists. While crows and ravens were once found mainly in rural areas, thus giving farmers the need to build scarecrows, they now can be found in great numbers in our urban areas. I've heard one of the reasons for this exodus is that streetlights enable them to watch for their most dangerous predator, the great horned owl. But the biggest reason is because of the readily available food in the form of litter and trash. They take advantage of Dumpsters, landfills, and discarded food containers. And my mother was right; they do eat carrion. *Corvidae* are known to be cannibalistic. They will eat the eggs and nestlings of other birds.

I came across an amazing example of this while reading Loren Eiseley's account from "The Judgment of the Birds." He was sleeping under a tree when he awoke to an awful scene.

> . . . and there on the extended branch sat an enormous raven with a red and squirming nestling in his beak.
>
> The sound that awoke me was the outraged cries of the nestling's parents, who flew helplessly in circles about the

---

[2]Ibid.

clearing. The sleek black monster was indifferent to them. He gulped, whetted his beak on the dead branch a moment and sat still. Up to that point the little tragedy had followed the usual pattern. But suddenly, out of all that area of woodland, a soft sound of complaint began to rise. Into the glade fluttered small birds of half a dozen varieties drawn by the anguished outcries of the tiny parents.

No one dared to attack the raven. But they cried there in some instinctive common misery, the bereaved and the unbereaved. The glade filled with their soft rustling and their cries. They fluttered as though to point their wings at the murderer. There was a dim intangible ethic he had violated, that they knew. He was a bird of death.

And he, the murderer, the black bird at the heart of life, sat on there, glistening in the common light, formidable, unmoving, unperturbed, untouchable.[3]

A stunning and awful scene, is it not? And yet, isn't this what you and I witness every day? Every night on the news we can watch innocent people being devoured by disease, robbery, rape, and murder. All the horrific stories that bombard us about atrocities in Bosnia, terrorists in Afghanistan, the World Trade Center attack, and a mother systematically drowning her five children in the bathtub don't make any sense. Sometimes it's all too hideous and I can't face the morning newspaper or the TV.

---

[3]From *The Immense Journey* by Loren Eiseley, copyright 1946, 1950, 1951, 1953, 1955, 1956, 1957 by Loren Eiseley. Used by permission of Random House, Inc.

Contrary to what some people would like us to believe, the world is *not* getting better. Even the newscasters were in agreement over September 11: there *is* evil in this world and we have seen it face-to-face. Sometimes this evil is in our own backyards in the form of adultery, betrayal, addictions, abuse, and death. What's our response supposed to be? How can we cope with this onslaught of evil? Is there any way to overcome it and not be crushed by it? Eiseley's story of the raven and what the birds did after their collective anguish over the nestlings' death gives us insight and an example.

> The sighing died. It was then I saw the judgment. It was the judgment of life against death. I will never see it again so forcefully presented. I will never hear of it again in notes so tragically prolonged. For in the midst of protest, they forgot the violence. There, in that clearing the crystal note of a song sparrow lifted hesitantly in the hush. And finally, after painful fluttering, another took the song, and then another, the song passing from one bird to another, doubtfully at first, as though some evil thing were being slowly forgotten. Till suddenly they took heart and sang from many throats joyously together as birds are known to sing. They sang because life is sweet and sunlight beautiful. They sang under the brooding shadow of the raven. In simple truth they had forgotten the raven, for they were the singers of life, and not of death.[4]

---

[4]Ibid.

After the horror and grief were expressed, the birds sang in praise of life. We too can be "singers of life, and not of death." In fact, therein lies the power to defeat darkness, in life-affirming songs of praise.

The Bible says, "But thou art holy, O thou that inhabitest the praises of Israel" (Psalm 22:3 KJV). God's presence and power are close at hand when we praise Him.

Just last month I had to go to a friend's funeral. She was in the prime of her life. Emily had gone through a nasty divorce and raised her three children by herself. Later she had met a wonderful man and they married. She had a successful business as an interior decorator, and she and her husband were one month away from moving into the dream home they had built. But the day before Valentine's Day, Emily was killed instantly in a freak accident. Her friends were stunned and shocked. *Emily? Dead?* It couldn't be! She was so vibrant, she lit up a room. She was so positive, she always had an encouraging word for everyone. Why her? Why didn't it happen to some jerk?

Somberly we all shuffled into the funeral service clutching our sodden handkerchiefs, our collective grief like an anvil on everyone's chest. But despite our grief, despite the anguish of none of it making sense, at her funeral we sang songs of hope. Tentatively at first, our voices grew and swelled in hope. We sang songs of the reality of a place where there is no pain, no death, and "God will wipe away every tear from their eyes" (Revelation 7:17).

After the terrorist attack on the World Trade
Center, my husband, Tom, was
stunned by what was happening a
few blocks away in Washington
Park. This is a park that we have
both walked through while visiting New York
City, and it is famous for drug dealing and drunks sprawled
everywhere—some urinating publicly. On the news, Tom
saw a different scene in Washington Park that night. Groups
of people were arm in arm, lighting candles, and singing
"Amazing Grace." Some confident, some quavering, the rag-
tag mix of outcasts and downtown workers lifted their voices
together, swayed, and warbled, "Through many dangers,
toils and snares I have already come; 'Tis grace that brought
me safe thus far. And grace will lead me home."[5] All over the
world people were gathering to light candles and sing songs
of hope and grace. Why?

Because singing and praising God lifts us out of our circumstances, pushes back the darkness, aligns us with His
resources, and says, "Evil will *not* have the last word. I will
not let it destroy me." Like the birds that "sang under the
brooding shadow of the raven," we can sing under the
brooding shadow of disappointment, death, or terrorist
attacks. Because life is sweet, we have hope for the future

---

[5]"Amazing Grace," John Newton.

and today we are here. Emily is not here. The people who perished in the World Trade Center are not here; maybe you have loved ones who are not here anymore. But *we* are here. We *can* rejoice. They would want us to.

~ *Sparrow* ~

I've never been a big fan of sparrows, or even given them much notice. Around the neighborhood pool where I grew up, they were as ubiquitous as mosquitoes. There were lots of kids running around the pool with crumbly snacks of popcorn, chips, and pretzels, and there were always lots of sparrows hopping around after them, cleaning up the bits with loud and eager chirps. If someone had asked me to describe a sparrow, I would have said, "Brown, eats trash." Although my mother would patiently teach me to identify the song of the cardinal, robin, and oriole, the sparrow wasn't discussed. The sparrow never registered as a bird that we should take notice of.

Decades later, I would still tell you that I'm not interested in sparrows. In fact, I have antagonistic feelings toward house sparrows. These sparrows—sometimes called English sparrows—are not natives. They were introduced to this country in 1850, and they compete with bluebirds and other natives for nesting spots. They are aggressive and often chase away the birds I *do* want in my nest boxes, even if they themselves can't fit in them.

In addition to their annoying habit of chasing away native birds, I can't think of anything noteworthy or special about them. Even Jesus refers to sparrows as quite common. In Matthew 10 and again in Luke He talks about how sparrows are sold for pennies. "Are not five sparrows sold for two pennies?" (Luke 12:6). I'm not sure why sparrows were sold, and I'm not sure I want to know. But the fact remains that they aren't rare or special. However, Jesus does go on to use the sparrow as an example of God's watchfulness and care over us. "Yet not one of them is forgotten by God. Indeed, the very hairs of your head are all numbered. Don't be afraid; you are worth more than many sparrows" (Luke 12:6–7).

I've heard these verses a million times, but I saw them in a new light when I got a personal demonstration and glimpse into God's heart—thanks to a lost sparrow the other day.

The pathetic little thing was lying by the door, *inside* on the carpet when I first spotted him. At first I was angry that Tom had left the door open, making it possible for wayward birds to get inside. But that emotion quickly turned to compassion and concern as I bent down to examine the confused little one that had lost his way.

Was he dead or just stunned? I couldn't tell. His eyes didn't blink and I couldn't see his breast move. To be safe, I got a magazine and tried to scoop him onto it so I could let him outside. Just as I was about to make contact with him, he sputtered to life and began to fly crazily about the room.

The house we have just moved into has vaulted ceilings two stories high and many windows. This is great for glimpses of the ocean but a nightmare for a trapped bird. A nightmare for me.

CRASH! Into the upper window he flew. *SMACK!* Feathers beat the air frantically as he bashed into another window, desperately seeking a way out of the unfamiliar place. With his every painful and frenzied attempt, my heart was twisting in pain for him. Dazed, he stopped for a moment on a high window ledge. Now I could see the rapid, frightened beating of his heart. I could sense his bewilderment and panic as each attempt left him more battered.

If only he'd stay still, I thought to myself. *Then I could catch him and rescue him from all this flailing around that's getting him nowhere.* I climbed up on the back of the sofa, teetering and maneuvering to get him off the high window ledge. As I edged my hands closer he took off again.

WHAM! Now he was erratically flying straight into blank

white walls. My breath caught with anxiety for him at each futile and potentially deadly attempt. "God!" I yelled as my eyes filled with tears of frustration and anger, "Why don't you *do* something?" Couldn't He see the plight of this little bird? Didn't He care?

The sparrow shook his head after his encounter with the wall and then zoomed across the room, straight for the glass doors. *BAM!* Down he dropped, into the corner he fell, behind the giant palm. *Did he finally break his neck?* I wondered. He was so beleaguered and so still. My heart ached in pity for him. I crept closer and closer, hoping to scoop him up in my hands. As I slowly drew near with my cupped hands only inches from him, he sputtered to consciousness and flew away from me. I muttered a discouraged oath under my breath.

By now I was about as panicked as the bird was. Sweat was pumping out of me from anxiety and exertion. Was I ever going to be able to get him out of here? (Was he going to poop all over the place?) Would he be too injured to survive when he finally *did* get out? Over and over I tried to help him, to rescue him from the torture he was inflicting on himself. But never would he trust me to take him to safety.

Despite my reservations that even more sparrows might come inside, I opened wide the door that he had initially come through. I had little hope that he would aim for it; the room was full of high windows and blank white walls that he kept choosing to smack into. And again he took a long, desperate attempt across the room at another white wall that he thought was a way out. *WHAM!* His frail little body made contact with the sky that wasn't there. Now up on a ledge thirteen feet high, he sat quietly. He was so still, I thought again that he was dead. He didn't even blink. *I* was blinking back even more tears as I felt the hopelessness and frustration of our predicament.

I wonder if God ever feels like this, I thought. *Does He feel this same amount of anguish for me when He sees me flailing about, confused and in pain?*

Growing up, if anybody had asked me in Sunday school about the emotions of God, I probably would have answered "anger." I had absorbed this through stories like the flood in Genesis, Sodom and Gomorrah, and the Israelites wandering forty years in the desert. Unfortunately, I didn't hear about His sorrow over the failure of people to trust Him, His hunger for our fellowship and sharing.

The New Testament tells us that Jesus is God with skin on, God among us, Emmanuel. Hebrews 1:3 says, "The Son is the radiance of God's glory and the exact representation of his being." So what emotions did Jesus show?

When Mary came and told Jesus that her brother, Lazarus, had died, He was not indifferent to her anguish. The Scriptures say "Jesus wept" (John 11:35). In Matthew, we see Jesus responding with compassion to the press of the crowds, not annoyance or detached piety. "When he saw the crowds, he had compassion on them, because they were harassed and helpless, like sheep without a shepherd" (Matthew 9:36). Not only does He have compassion for us; He loves us. "This is love: not that we loved God, but that he loved us and sent his Son as an atoning sacrifice for our sins. . . . And so we know and rely on the love God has for us. God is love. Whoever lives in love lives in God, and God in him" (1 John 4:10, 16). Clearly, our God is a God of compassion, caring, and love. So why do bad things happen to innocent sparrows? Or to you and me?

While I would prefer a genie god, one who will rescue me out of calamity and heartache whenever I need it, that's not who God is. (And I've noticed that throughout the Bible, miraculous works by God don't guarantee a person's heart is changed; just follow the antics of the Israelites in the desert.) Although I've read several excellent books about the mystery of suffering and why God heals or doesn't heal people, I don't think anyone this side of heaven is able to give me the definitive answer.[1]

What brings me comfort and solace is knowing that God is not indifferent to my sufferings. He knows, He cares, and He weeps. I remember one time sitting in my car at a stoplight. I was so frustrated and angry with God over His silence in my life and that He wasn't fixing things that I knew in His sovereignty He *could* fix. I saw Him answer

---

[1] Philip Yancey's *Disappointment With God* (Zondervan Publishing House, 1988) is a great book that addresses these questions. So is Jerry Bridges' *Trusting God Even When Life Hurts* (Navpress, 1988).

other people's prayers; why not mine? I banged my fists on the dashboard and yelled, "I feel so *abandoned* by you!" Then I remembered Jesus and I thought, *You're in good company, then, aren't you?* Life is unfair. It was unfair to the greatest and only perfect One who walked this earth, Jesus Christ. For all His compassion, healing, and generosity, He was nailed to a Roman cross. "Why have you forsaken me?" was His anguished cry. Why do I expect to get special treatment and escape hard times? I don't have all the answers, but I do have a game plan.

I can be an agent of change. I can turn my angst into something positive. I can seek to give compassion and solace to those around me who are suffering. Having gone through hard times myself, I know now that the best thing I can say to one in pain is not a Bible verse or "I know just how you feel" but "I'm so sorry. This must be incredibly difficult for you." It's not my job to solve it or make them feel better. I know that sometimes people just need to air their grief, and it's not my job to shame or correct them on every angry and heretical thing they say in the venting of their grief. The fellowship of a silent and listening presence is a tangible and powerful witness of God's love to an aching heart.

I sat on the couch with the door wide open and contemplated these things. As I looked out onto the porch and watched the other birds out there on the feeders, I felt a *whoosh* graze the top of my head. My little sparrow must have perked up to the calls of his friends outside. He flew straight

out through the open door and into freedom, seemingly in fine shape for the journeys ahead.

It was surprising to me how much my heart ached over that little lost sparrow. Although I didn't like or care about sparrows, I was driven to heart-pounding concern and tears over him. He was vulnerable, lost, and terribly frightened. His quest became my quest. I wanted to move heaven and earth to help him find his way out. God says He not only likes but loves us and cares for us deeply. We are worth much more than a little sparrow. I hope the next time I'm feeling lost, panicked, and frantic, I remember that my heavenly Father's heart is aching too. He longs to help, and just maybe He's trying to get my attention. If only I'd stop flying around in a frenzy long enough to remember the words to that hymn, *His eye is on the sparrow, and I know He watches me.*

～ *Mockingbird* ～

It was my father's birthday and I was on the last flight out of Chicago's O'Hare airport to my parents' home. As usual for that airline and that airport, my connecting flight was cancelled. I was livid and heartbroken. "You can't just abandon a whole planeload of people," I wailed to the ticket agent. (Oh yes, they can.) "And besides, it's my father's *birthday*. I've *got* to get home." My pathetic hard-luck story did me no good. She just gave me a tight-lipped smile that said *Too bad, honey* and handed me a voucher for the airport hotel to stay the night. I determined they were not going to ruin my trip and looked around for alternatives. Then I noticed the two gregarious businessmen standing near me in the same situation.

Their names were Frank and Jim, and they began to joke and commiserate with me. "This airline is awful; they *always* strand us here," said Jim. Good, I wasn't alone in my misery. But then they made me nervous. "Ride with us!" Frank invited cheerfully. "We've rented a car." *You've got to be kidding,* I thought. Ride with two men who are complete strangers, late at night? Why not just tell me you're Charles Manson's brothers? It had the same appeal.

Then another woman, about fifty years old, seemingly sane and sensibly attired, approached us. "Hi, my name's Anne and I'd like to join you," she said. I turned to her in shock, "*What?* You're willing to ride with these guys who are complete strangers, in a confined car?"

"Sure," she said, "I've taken rides several times before. This isn't the first time this airline has stranded me. Join us; you'll be safe." She looked normal; they looked normal, so I said yes. A couple hours later, I remembered that looks can be deceiving.

I always try to avoid discussions about politics and religion, especially when I'm in the company of strangers. I was only going to be with these people for a few hours, so why rock the boat? But I couldn't avoid it when they brought it up.

"How do you two guys know each other?" I asked.

Frank answered, "We go way back . . . known each other for about twenty years. We work as contractors on exclusive and upscale homes. We're designing a house out here in the Midwest, but we're from the East Coast. And we met because a friend introduced us to the same guru."

Here we go, I thought.

"Guru?" I said. "Tell me more about him."

Jim went on to describe how this guru's wisdom surpassed anything he had ever witnessed. "He changed my life. He was just so—so *wise*. I've never met anyone like him in my life." He began to describe to me things he had learned from his guru about the universe and infinity. Fortunately, because my husband has a Ph.D. in physics and we have talked about some of these things, I could smell the cow dung clinging to his theories and sense when Jim was talking himself into a circle. He also talked about how they buried the followers in a certain way so they could have the right foods to eat and come up-out of their graves when they were reincarnated. After about a thirty-minute soliloquy on how incredibly *wise* and *awesome* this guru was, I asked him a question.

"So, what other religions or philosophies have you explored and how has this guru changed your life?"

"I didn't need to explore any further—he had all the answers! He taught me how we all just need to *love* each other to achieve oneness. He taught me about the importance of meditation, how through this meditation we can bring about *world peace,* and the importance of cleansing myself from all material wants. . . ." I wanted to but didn't ask, *Were there not enough people meditating for world peace September 11? If you're free from material wants, then why do you charge so much?*

The conversation turned to other religions. Anne volunteered that she had been the victim of a nasty divorce and thought all organized religion was "crap." She was, however, enthralled by their guru. We attempted to talk about Mohammed, Buddha, and Eastern religions for a while, but they hadn't studied anything else and so didn't have any other opinions to offer.

This drives me crazy. If someone is going to say, "I've found the answer to life and truth," then I would hope he has explored some options, studied history, read up on great thinkers. When I was exploring other religions, agnosticism, and atheism, I looked up biographies of the people who espoused these ideas. I researched the history of several religions. I don't mind if someone has a different viewpoint than I do, but I was disappointed that they hadn't put much thought into it. At least we could have had a stimulating conversation. All they knew was their backwoods guru.

Then I asked, "What do you all think about Jesus Christ?"

"He was a good person, a great teacher," said Jim. "Just another prophet, though."

"Actually," I said, "He didn't leave you that option. He

said that He was the Son of God, equal to God, and He was the only way to heaven.[1] If He said that and He was *lying* or delusional, then He can't be a good moral teacher. He's either who He said He was or a liar or a nutcase."

"Awww, Jesus never said those things!" said Jim. He went on to describe how his guru explained that we ascribe all sorts of sayings to Jesus that weren't necessarily true. His guru had spent a lot of time revealing to him who Jesus *really* was. (His guru had apparently gotten all this information by personal revelation via meditation.) I always find it fascinating how people can talk calmly about Mohammed or other prophets, but when the name of *Jesus* is brought up, things start to heat up.

I tried to demonstrate that there were more archaeological evidence and eyewitness accounts to the facts of Jesus' life and resurrection than there were to the fact that Julius Caesar had ever existed. But they wouldn't hear any of it. Not only did they shut down when presented with the facts, they got hostile. They didn't want to hear anything different from their opinions. They didn't want to ask any questions. They preferred to mimic an old guru's opinions and defend them vigorously. We decided to move on to different topics.

Like Frank and Jim, when it comes to living out our

---

[1] "I and the Father are one" (John 10:30). "I am the way and the truth and the life. No one comes to the Father except through me" (John 14:6). "Anyone who has seen me has seen the Father" (John 14:9). "They all asked, 'Are you then the Son of God?' He replied, 'You are right in saying I am'" (Luke 22:70).

beliefs, a lot of us behave like the mockingbird. The mockingbird is a fantastic mimic. Its Latin name is *Mimus polyglottos*. *Mimus* is Latin for "a mimic" and *polyglottos* is Greek for "many tongued." Native Americans in South Carolina called this bird *the one with four hundred tongues*. They've been known to imitate other bird songs as well as rusty hinges, baby cries, dog barks, and cellular phones. A mockingbird can imitate as many as thirty-two other species within ten minutes. My friend Tracie tells me about a mockingbird around her house that imitates car alarms. Like Frank and Jim, the mockingbird is influenced greatly by the company he keeps. Once the mockingbird migrates from South America after the winter, ornithologists have witnessed scraps of bird songs indigenous to that area coming out of the mockingbird's repertoire.

Although the mockingbird looks unassuming (he's about eleven inches long, gray with a lighter underside and gray and white wings), he is a vigorous defender of his territory. He is so well known for this that legend has it Texas chose the mockingbird for its state bird because the bird is "a fighter for the protection of his home, falling, if need be, in its defense, like any true Texan." (This is the state that has bumper stickers that read, "Don't Mess With Texas.") The mockingbird will defend his territory against all comers—

other birds, dogs, and cats—and will even dive-bomb humans who get too close.

Like Frank and Jim, you and I aren't too different in behavior from the mockingbird either, if you think about it. Most of us mimic our parents' political persuasion; we mimic the way our families vote. Many of us, if we attend church, go to the same denomination or type of church our parents did. We listen to talk shows that mimic our beliefs. We choose to surround ourselves with people who think the way we do. That makes us comfortable. We mimic their actions, beliefs, and words. We are, by and large, mimics of the people who have influenced us. And God help anybody who challenges us on our opinions or beliefs. Many a dinner party (or car trip) is ruined when different opinions on religion and politics are raised.

It's so easy to mimic the motions of faith from those around us rather than to think things through for ourselves and live authentic lives. It's so easy to mimic and look like upstanding members of the community while our lives are unraveling. So many of us refuse to give up our secret addictions, our pursuit of material one-upmanship, and our false fronts of having it all together. We mimic the look and actions of what "successful" people are doing so we can be perceived that way too. That's why I found it so refreshing the night I went with my friend to her twelve-step group.

There were no masks in the room that night. Instead of mimicking the local high-tech-I'm-going-somewhere-stock-options talk, people were saying what was true. "Hi, I'm Jean and I'm a bulimic. I can't stop gorging and throwing up food. I need your prayers." Or, "Hi, I'm John and I'm a rage-aholic. I need help." And, "Hi, I'm Sue and I can't stop cutting myself until I bleed." Each person's confession was greeted with acceptance and warmth and love. They reminded me of the story in Luke between the Pharisee (religious leader) and the publican (everyday guy—a tax collector who skimmed off the top).

To some who were confident of their own righteousness and looked down on everybody else, Jesus told this parable: "Two men went up to the temple to pray, one a Pharisee and the other a tax collector. The Pharisee stood up and prayed about himself: 'God, I thank you that I am not like other men—robbers, evildoers, adulterers—or even like this tax collector. I fast twice a week and give a tenth of all I get.'

"But the tax collector stood at a distance. He would not even look up to heaven, but beat his breast and said, 'God, have mercy on me, a sinner.'

"I tell you that this man, rather than the other, went home justified before God. For everyone who exalts himself will be humbled, and he who humbles himself will be exalted" (Luke 18:9–14).

If we are to mimic anybody, according to Jesus, we should not look to the religious rulers or people who think they have it all together. He was not impressed with the religious leader's attitude of *Thank God I'm not like these other slobs who lie, steal, and commit acts of perversion*. But Jesus was impressed by the humble man who knew he was a sinner and dependent upon the love and grace of God. To Jesus, the self-righteous religious leader was the perverse one. In fact, Jesus said the main reason he was so disgusted with the Pharisees was because "Everything they do is done for men to see" (Matthew 23:5). He doesn't want everyone mimicking a holier-than-thou attitude and living lives full of religious activity but devoid of compassion. Like Holden Caulfield in *The Catcher in the Rye*, Jesus is not impressed by phonies.

While watching the folks in the twelve-step program, I thought to myself, *Isn't this what the church is supposed to be about?* Aren't we supposed to be mimicking Jesus' love and forgiveness? There may be exceptions, but it would be rare to walk into a church and hear people talking this way. Doesn't it seem we're more often tempted to mimic some Hollywood myth of the perfect life and vigorously defend our right to live lives free of accountability?

While we enjoy telling other people what moral code they should live by, the fact is Christians have the same divorce rate as non-churchgoers. While many believers in this country are obese (thirty pounds overweight or more), we don't weep and wail over the starving children in the world—even our own country—although there is plenty of food and money to feed them. Instead, we focus on the sins of people with "alternative lifestyles" and cluck our tongues at them. We don't pray over expensive purchases we want, but we're quick to *tsk-tsk* the exorbitant spending of others when they buy sports cars or mansions.

Why do we do this? Why do we focus on others, those who don't even proclaim to believe the things we do, instead of taking the log out of our own eyes and making our own lives accountable before God? I think it's largely because of the company we keep. We want to be accepted; we want to be in the fold. We don't want others to doubt our standing before God, so we mimic the God-talk and attitudes of those around us without thinking things through for ourselves. During Bill Clinton's moral failures, I eagerly listened to Christian talk shows that criticized and condemned the man. I should have, instead, been praying for him. Instead of shaking our heads at what "they" are doing outside our churches, we should be seeing what we can do.

Why don't we mimic Jesus and find ways to alleviate the sufferings of the poor? (Because, privately, we think they are lazy.) Why don't we adopt orphans who need families? (Because we don't want to be inconvenienced.) Why don't we look for ways to *serve* instead of how we can pass judgment on others' lifestyles? When Christians line up to serve at our local homeless shelters, soup kitchens, and AIDS hospices, that's when the world will sit up, take notice, and want to find out more about this God we believe in. Instead, the world sees Christians huddling in their ghettos and casting judgment on others in their suffering. Here is the kind of behavior God wants us to mimic: "Religion that God our Father accepts as pure and faultless is this: to look after orphans and widows in their distress and to keep oneself from being polluted by the world" (James 1:27). The emphasis is looking out for the powerless and downtrodden of society and not going with the flow. Not getting caught up in the current frenzy of materialism. Most Christian women I know (including myself) don't think twice about going shopping or to the mall every day. Just for fun. I'm bothered by the fact that in the Western world we are drowning in luxury and consuming most of the world's resources while the rest of the world is scraping by for a decent meal.

Our friends Jack and Terry have found a creative and simple way to serve (among many that they practice). When they travel they try to rent motel rooms a couple steps down from what they can afford and give the money they saved to charity. This makes me squirm. I'm too busy always making sure I'm comfortable. When Tom and I are on vacation, I want the best room we can afford—and with a view. I don't give a thought about the homeless people a few blocks away. I can't save the world, but I could make simple choices like

Jack and Terry the next time I travel and serve others that way.

In the book *To Kill a Mockingbird*, the young girl named Scout is told that "It's a sin to kill a mockingbird" because "mockingbirds don't do one thing but make music for us to enjoy . . . but sing their hearts out for us. That's why it's a sin to kill a mockingbird." Hopefully, people will feel the same way about criticizing Christians, because we'll be known for mimicking Jesus, singing our hearts out for others through lives of service.

~ Hummingbird ~

I love to watch the hummingbirds at our feeders. With their brilliant colors of ruby and emerald, they look like jewels as they dart around in the sunshine. They seem to defy the laws of physics the way they zip about and hover. The first time I saw one up close I was watering some plants with the hose in my garden. Suddenly I heard this unearthly buzzing sound next to my ear. I thought it was some gigantic prehistoric bee or hungry locust, so I screamed and swatted at it. Then I saw that it was only a curious hummingbird, hovering close by to get a better look at me. I felt remorse that I had frightened it away with my wild movements but resolved that it wouldn't happen again. Next time I heard what sounds like a miniature helicopter next to my ear, I'd turn slowly toward it.

A couple of days later I had my chance. I was holding the hose so that the spray arched up and down, a sort of rainbow of water. I wasn't moving because I was deep in thought. Suddenly a hummingbird flew into the spray right in front of me. He was a brilliant kaleidoscope of movement. His throat was a deep fuchsia pink that shimmered in the sun. His little green body looked metallic as he pirouetted and danced in the water spray. After a while, he flew up to my face and hovered there for a minute, his little wings humming a low roar in my ears. He seemed to be trying to communicate something to me. Or at least giving me a definite acknowledgment of my presence and his gratefulness for the shower. Then he went back down into the spray of water and flitted and danced some more. Finally he hovered underneath the spray and opened his beak wide. He was happily letting the spray wash over him and drinking in the water at the same time. He took several long drinks of water. Then, just as suddenly as he appeared, he was gone.

Since then, I've learned their birdcalls and can now recognize them even if I don't see them. When the feeder is low, they sound like they are chiding me for depriving them of their favorite drink.

I bought my feeder at a Wild Birds Unlimited store, and I recommend this chain highly. They are devoted to helping

people attract birds to backyard feeders. The stores are
staffed with knowledgeable
people who can recommend
exactly the right type of bird seed for
the bird you hope to attract.[1]

I had seen pictures of hummingbird feeders
where the nectar was red due to food coloring.
This is not recommended anymore and is not necessary for attracting hummingbirds. The birds are
attracted to the bright red color of the *feeder*, not to the liquid,
and the artificial coloring is not good for them. The correct
mixture for hummingbird nectar is one part white sugar to
four parts water, so I mix a half a cup of sugar and two cups
of water. My feeder is round with six feeding holes in it.
This, I think, is a joke.

I noticed that the hummingbirds at our feeders are
extremely territorial. They will not share the feeder with any
other hummingbird and are adamant about that. So when I
saw photos in my Wild Birds Unlimited store of several
hummingbirds peacefully drinking from the same feeder, I
felt cheated. Then I found out that here, near the California
coast, our hummingbirds (black-chinned, Anna's, Costa's,
and Allen's) are much more territorial than the Eastern
ruby-throated. What I do get instead are amazing displays of
fighter-pilot maneuvers.

---

[1]*www.wbu.com.*

These hummingbirds put on spectacular U-shaped diving displays. They rise to 120 feet, then dive down at speeds up to 65 miles per hour and veer up at the bottom making a loud *keeeaaaak* sound. If another hummingbird comes into the garden and dares to try to drink at the feeder, even more theatrical displays appear. The defending hummingbird will dive-bomb the intruder and they both will zoom around the yard so fast and fly straight up so high that our eyes can't follow them. It's like having our own miniature Blue Angels show.

Despite watching them zoom down from the trees and dart about the garden, I've never seen a nest. I figured it would be next to impossible to see one because they're often smaller than the leaves on the tree. The nests are about the size of a golf ball, just big enough to hold the usual two eggs at half an inch long each—about the size of a kidney bean. I've often tried to follow the hummingbirds with my eyes as they go into the shrubs and trees, but the nests are just too small to spot. I thought about this the other morning as I watched them from my desk, hovering around the feeder, before I had to turn my attention back to the computer, the bills, and other pressing matters.

 There's a lot going on in our lives right now, so I've been talking to God more than usual throughout the day. "Why hasn't our house sold yet?" I ask Him. "Should we take it off the market? Is

the timing wrong? Do you want us not to sell, or are we being too greedy?" And I wonder about my husband's job. "Is his company going to suffer this downsizing that's going on around us in Silicon Valley?" I wonder about having kids. "Am I too old? Would this be too taxing for me? What do you want us to do?" But sometimes it feels like God's too busy in the Middle East or another "hot spot" and isn't attending to my requests when I want Him to. Like, right *now*.

Fortunately for me, God's got a sense of humor and isn't limited by time, physics, or my bad attitude. The day after talking to Him about these things and my internal hummingbird musings, I went outside for the morning paper.

There, lying right next to the morning news, was a perfectly formed hummingbird nest. I was stunned. It must have fallen out of the tree above the driveway, but it looked like somebody (or God's angel) had carefully laid it there. It was exquisite.

I called my sister and told her about it and she said, "Laurie, I have friends who have studied birds for *years* and have never seen one because they are so small and rare to find."

It felt as though God was winking at me and saying, "I know the desires of your heart, even those that you don't speak out loud. I know everything and I am totally in control. I can make anything 'drop' into your lap whenever I want . . . hummingbird nests, jobs, or house sales."

Despite his pain and suffering, Job said, "I know that you can do all things; no plan of yours can be thwarted."[2] I look at my hummingbird nest now and smile. It is physical proof to me that Job was right and that nothing is impossible with God.

---

[2]Job 42:2.

~ *Oriole* ~

I used to be so jealous of my next-door neighbor. I felt like a bag lady compared to her. While I would run to the store at a moment's notice in sweat pants and no makeup, she would never deign to leave her front doorstep without being properly attired. This usually consisted of a tasteful Ralph Lauren designer outfit, perfect hair, flawless skin, and neat baskets for each errand. I didn't have orderly baskets for each errand. I tossed plastic bags in the backseat of the car in my mad rush to get to the store.

Not only did she always look perfect, her home was perfect. While ours still looked like the 1950s-era house it originally was, hers had been gutted and groomed. She had cathedral ceilings, new double-paned windows, French antiques, a new kitchen, and a master suite with French doors that led out to a pool area. No matter what time of day or year you stopped by, it was always immaculate—and she had two kids. My house, on the other hand, frequently looked like a couple of teenagers had just blown through. But it was only me (and my endless projects) and Tom living there. I alternated between wanting to learn from her and wanting to push her into a mud hole. Even her garden was tightly manicured and perfect. Is it any wonder that the other neighbors and I jokingly referred to her as Pauline the Perfect?

The bird world has its Pauline the Perfect too, and her name is the oriole. I don't know if the other songbirds are jealous or not, but they have plenty of reasons to be.

There are several different orioles in North America: orchard, hooded, Baltimore, Bullock's, and Scott's orioles. (Well, there are more, but they are in small, isolated places that most people won't see.) For our purposes, I am referring to the Bullock's oriole (seen in the West) and Baltimore oriole (seen in the East). They are the most common and are similar in appearance.

These birds stand out in a crowd; few can catch attention compared to the colorful drama of the oriole. Not only do they have a lovely song, they are brightly painted in orange, black, and white. Their breasts are vivid orange, their heads are black, and their wings are streaked with black and white.

The most unusual aspect of the orioles is not their coloring, however. Like my elegant neighbor, it is their *home* that is so special. The fantastic engineering feat of the orioles' suspended, pendulous nest is what distinguishes them from other songbirds.

When the females arrive in the spring, they begin building the long, woven sacklike nest hanging from the end of a drooping branch. I would love to see a slow-motion video of this, because it is such an amazing feat of engineering skill. I don't think I could replicate it even with a crochet hook or knitting needles. How the oriole manages with just a beak confounds me. When she's finished building it, she's intricately woven plant bits, horsehair, grasses, and mosses into a nest that seems to defy the laws of physics.

Not only is the nest itself unique, but where she builds it is also a smart move. Hanging precariously from a flimsy, drooping branch (often over a road), it presents an effective barrier from predators trying to climb along the branch to reach the nest. Despite its vulnerable look, it is quite sturdy. Summer storms do not budge it. In fact, you usually don't notice an oriole's nest until the fall, when all the leaves drop off the trees. I've seen a nest only once. It was the onset of winter and there was an old nest in a neighbor's tree. I'd walked by that spot many times, but I had never noticed the well-hidden construction marvel.

It's not difficult to attract these talented and beautiful birds to your backyard. Just put out some orange halves or a sugar solution in an oriole feeder (this is similar to a hummingbird feeder, but it has bigger holes and is orange in color).

Like the other songbirds in the vicinity of the talented and beautiful oriole, I am surrounded by talented and beautiful people in the Silicon Valley. Frequently, I find myself in the company of women who have silicone chests, immaculate faces, and showplace homes. I remember at one New Year's Eve dinner at my sister's house, all of the women (except two of us) were wearing necklaces of black pearls the size of walnuts. I started to crave and desire a black pearl necklace for myself. Never mind that I would have hardly any occasion to wear it; the current fashion and their lustrous opalescent beauty dazzled me.

Whenever I walk into one of those women's designer showplace homes, I am consumed by the need to upgrade (or dump) my own. Their immaculate and perfectly coordinated rooms filled with antiques and *objets d'art* make me feel like I'm missing out. It doesn't matter that I have a very nice home that makes people feel warm and comfortable; my vision and focus are suddenly filled with what I don't have. Our culture too, with its billboards, TV, and print ads, is geared toward making us feel that we need more. It seems so natural that we don't realize how seriously God views this coveting and envy of what others have.

The story of Adam and Eve in Genesis shows the disastrous consequences of taking our eyes off the blessings God has bestowed on us. They had everything they needed or wanted. Any fruit they could eat, except for one. Of course, the one thing they didn't have is what filled their vision. Eve focused in on the *one thing* she couldn't have instead of all her other blessings. In the book of John we see Jesus' response to wasting our time pondering others' fates: "Peter turned and saw that the disciple whom Jesus loved was following them. (This was the one who had leaned back against Jesus at the supper and had said, 'Lord, who is going to betray you?') When Peter saw him, he asked, 'Lord, what about him?' Jesus answered, 'If I want him to remain alive until I return, what is that to you? You must follow me'" (John 21:20–22).

Tom keeps pointing out to me that our desire for more is as simple as breaking the tenth commandment. "You shall not covet your neighbor's house. You shall not covet your neighbor's wife [or husband] . . . or anything that belongs to your neighbor" (Exodus 20:17). I take the other commandments seriously (not worshiping any idols above God, not killing, and so on) but somehow I've got it into my head that coveting isn't all that serious. But it *is* serious, and it has serious consequences. I begin to feel unhappy, restless, and miserable. I start to focus on all the things I think will make me happier. In effect, I curse and forget all the wonderful blessings I do have.

For years I've kept a journal, and I never felt more strongly motivated to write in it than when I was miserable. Hence, most entries were filled with what was going wrong in my life, how discontented I was, and how I wished my circumstances or people around me would change. I realized one day that if I died suddenly and someone read my journals, they would conclude that I either was a very morose person or I didn't really know Jesus Christ and His blessings. So I decided to change this. Now I have a separate journal in which I write only positive things. I write down answers to prayer. I concentrate on my blessings; I focus in on what's wonderful in my life.

Tom and I have done this in our prayer walks as well. We used to start out repeating to God our long lists of requests. These aren't always selfish things; most of the time they are for others' well-being and health. Still, we weren't focusing on our blessings. We decided to start out our walks by speaking only praises to God. Thanking Him not only for the blessings He's given us but also for who He is. His creativity, His eternal love, His compassion. Then, when we turn around to head home, we start on the list of prayer requests. At first, it was embarrassingly difficult to think of things to keep praising God for when we were so used to our grocery list of needs. But after a while it became a joyful, uplifting, and easy thing to do.

Scripture is full of texts that show us that this change of focus is the key to contentment and peace. Isaiah 26:3 says having our minds fully focused on and trusting in God will keep us in "perfect peace." And Hebrews 13:5 states, "Keep your lives free from the love of money and be content with what you have, because God has said, 'Never will I leave you; never will I forsake you.' "

The barn swallow doesn't waste her time contemplating how to build a nest like the oriole. That wouldn't suit her purposes. She needs to be under a barn eave, stuck up against a wall in a secure mud nest, close to her supply of insects. God has given her the exact talent she needs. The oriole doesn't waste her time trying to emulate the barn swallow. We waste time focusing on what others have instead of what God is doing with us today. Jesus said He cares for the sparrows and pointed out their freedom from worry. He told us to do the same. So no matter what our circumstances are, no matter what others around us possess, no matter how elegantly attired our friends are or how perfect their homes, we can choose to be rich in peace and contentment—no matter how much like Pauline the Perfect our neighbors are.

~ *Goldfinch* ~

Invaders have come into our remote, lovely country property that we hope to develop one day. I hate them. Beginning in spring, I crane my neck searching for them as we drive up the mountain. I squint into the distance to see if any new groups of them have multiplied. I furtively look around for them on each morning walk. Instead of beholding the emerging wild flowers or listening for the wrens, I'm focusing on whether or not there seem to be more of them. Because they are uninvited and unwanted, I sputter in indignation, I complain, growl, and whimper to Tom when I see them. "Look!" I whine, "I tell you, I think there are *twice* as many this time!" He is sick of listening to me. "Nuke them already!" he says. They are big, tough, and aggressive. They are thistles.

When we first bought the property three years ago, there weren't any. Well, there were lots of them five miles down at the bottom of the mountain, but they weren't in *our* back-yard. Now they are starting to form a welcoming committee up and down the sides of the road on our parcel. They taunt and wave at me as we drive past. They don't have mere prickles but inch-long barbs that threaten me as I walk by. Miniature fields of them are spreading over the indigo-blue wild lupine. At first I blamed the local rancher. We regularly let his cows graze on our property, and I was convinced they were eating thistles and spreading them in their cow pies. But my neighbor Wayne says it's the roadwork that does it.

Every year we have someone come up and maintain the road. He does grading and repair work, plus he lays down a layer of crushed rock. He also spreads thistle seeds he has picked up from other places in the county.

If I weren't so well-rounded in my obsessions, I'd make a perfect obsessive-compulsive. I fixate on these thistles. I don't care if it's ninety degrees outside, I'm doggedly out there with a shovel, muttering curses under my breath as the sweat pours down my face while I try to dig out these thorny and prolific invaders. After I dig them out, I gingerly place them in huge black plastic lawn bags. I don't want the seeds to spread. Considering the number of plants I am able to dig up versus the hordes multiplying like an aggressive virus, it's easy to get overwhelmed and discouraged.

Wayne gave me a tempting offer to "nuke" them as Tom suggested. "I'm spraying Roundup on the thistles at our place. You want me to do yours too?" I bite my lip in consideration; I am sorely tempted. The Monsanto Company says Roundup breaks down immediately into the ground and doesn't do any lasting damage to the soil, surrounding plants, or habitat. Many organic organizations[1] and magazines say they have the science to prove that's not the case. They say Roundup isn't as safe as it's purported to be. I want to be a responsible steward of our property. I don't want to introduce deadly chemicals that will harm the

[1]These Web sites explain why Roundup may not be as safe as you think: www.geocities.com/organic_gardener/roundup.html and www.greenpeaceusa.org/media/factsheets.

ground-nesting birds, the butterflies, the rodent-eating
snakes, and the wild flowers. But I
do want to end our thistle plague. I
hedge, mutter, and say, "I'll think
about it." Tom rolls his eyes.

Months later, in late summer,
we come back to the mountain and begin our ascent. The air
is warm and dry; red dust billows behind us as we climb. I
look out the window and begin my ritual assessment of
whether the thistle invasion seems to be spreading. Despite
my hatred and loathing of the noxious plants, I find myself
admiring the brilliant purple blooms they now display. Some
are huge, four-inch pompons bowing a welcome in the after-
noon sun. I notice something else: the thistles are attracting
goldfinches. Hundreds of gorgeous, dazzling goldfinches
flutter about in a confetti of sunshine. It's as if some giddy
decorator from Ringling Brothers Circus orchestrated the
pairing of these taxicab-yellow finches against the throbbing
purple blossoms. They dance together in happy reciprocity.

The American goldfinch is attracted to thistles for both
food and the fluffy down the plants produce when they are
finished flowering. The birds use this down to line their
nests with a cozy layer of white fluff. After eating the thistle
seeds, goldfinches regurgitate the seeds from their crops to
feed both their mates who are incubating eggs and the baby
nestlings once they have hatched. Spring is the best time to

spot the male goldfinch because he goes
through two molts per year. In the fall
after breeding he undergoes a complete
molt of all his feathers and then again there is
a partial molt in early spring. At these stages,
he looks more like the olive-ish drab female
goldfinch. Late spring and summer are the
best times to spot him, and it won't be difficult. After his
early spring molt, he is a bright, intense yellow with black
and white wings and a small black cap—almost like a
beret—on the top of his head.

I started to think twice about obliterating the goldfinches' favorite food source. I thought about how nice it
would be to see them every morning, carrying the sunshine
on their backs no matter what the weather was doing. I
thought about how the food source of the gaily-colored Carolina parakeet was obliterated, and now they are extinct. I
thought about how often good things come to me in prickly
packages I normally would not care to receive.

When I met Tom, although I was fascinated by our con-
versations, I summarily crossed him off my list as a potential
mate. He wasn't the package I was looking for. I didn't want
a divorced man. But what I got was a sensitive, caring soul,
acquainted with grief and so mindful to the importance of
communication. I didn't want stepchildren (even if they were
young adults); I wanted my *own* children. But what I got was
the gift of warmth, love, and friendship I was hungering for

and needed. I didn't want a husband thirteen years older than me, but what I got was a man who was confident and secure and didn't need to run around trying to prove himself. (I knew he was The Man when we were dating and I said to him in a moment of haughtiness and self-importance, "Actually, Tom, I was looking for someone a little younger." He sighed and said with a smile, "Yeah, so was I.")

Moses had to lead a prickly and contentious people through the desert. If they had been easily led and followed directions, Moses wouldn't have learned to rely on a God who could and would deliver on His promises. David was anointed king but then had to run for his life from the prickly King Saul, who was jealous and wanted to kill him. The position of king came in a package of running for his life and learning to have faith. He wouldn't have developed a closer relationship with God unless he accepted the conditions. The psalmist said, "It was good for me to be afflicted so that I might learn your decrees" (Psalm 119:71) and also, "You hear, O Lord, the desire of the afflicted; you encourage them, and you listen to their cry" (Psalm 10:17). There is a familiar saying, "Everyone wants to get to heaven, but nobody wants to die." We want the gifts and prizes but we don't like the tough conditions and packages they come in. We don't like to die to our demands and dreams about the way we think things *should* or *ought* to be.

My friend Diana didn't want the incurable disease of MS, but her condition forces her to slow down and take

breaks. Now she has more opportunity to pray for loved ones and contemplate heavenly matters, something she didn't have time for when she was rushing around and checking things off her to-do list.

I didn't want the six years of health-related heartaches that leveled my pride and dreams for the future. But I learned about endurance and steadfastness. I learned compassion for others who can't avail themselves of a quick fix. I learned how painful the unasked-for pat answer or scriptural bandage can be. I've learned to focus on the many, many things I have to be grateful for and not focus on the few things that are denied me. And through it all, I am becoming more the person I wanted to be all along. Many of life's beautiful gifts and lessons come in prickly packages that we'd rather not open. But through them we can discover the symbiosis between the pain and joy of relinquishment that unveils heaven's priceless gifts.

～ Wren ～

When I met Tom, I was thirty, jobless, and living in a garage. It's not as bad as it sounds; it was in a very beautiful community, and the elderly woman who owned the place had turned a small portion of her garage into a studio apartment. But as my Australian friends would say, "It wasn't big enough in there to swing a cat." It was cramped, but I tried to think of it as cozy. It was fine in the summer but bone-chilling cold and damp in the winter. I had to have two electric heaters on full blast in order to stop shivering under my down comforter. Plus, the toilet wasn't inside the apartment; it was in a separate closet in the garage. This made for an eye-opening experience to creep out there in the cold, dark night and sit down on that icy seat. I looked forward to having a more normal home in the future.

When I married Tom we lived in the home he had bought before we met. It had a great layout, but it was very close to a freeway. A *loud* freeway. Since it was about fifty years old with structural changes that weren't to code, it was in constant need of repair. Sometimes it felt like I had a secondary job, keeping that house running. Plus, after our dog died, we started having a rodent problem under the house. They never got *inside* the house, but when they expired under the house, the smell was enough to drive us *out* of the house. I was relieved when we sold it. Now we're renting a place and I'm dreaming about building a home.

I thought this would be a time of bliss and happy planning. (I knew what I didn't want—outdoor toilets and crawl spaces for rodents.) Instead, I find myself tortured and paralyzed by indecision. Since I plan to be taken out of this home about forty-five years from now, feet first with a sheet over my head, I want it to be *perfect*. I'll have to live with the decisions I make now for the rest of my life.

I started gathering advice from everyone. My sister swears by her indestructible tiled kitchen floor. Others tell me my back will be screaming at me if I do that—I should choose wood. I'd like to frame the house in steel, but the contractor and my husband think I'm silly. "Wood is fine," they tell me. Granite counter tops would be nice, but I think tile is more our budget. However, our rental home has tile and I hate the way the grout catches all the spilled food. I notice that some redone kitchens have poured-concrete counter tops. Maybe we should try that. One story or two? L-shaped kitchen with island or U-shaped without? Decisions, decisions—my head is spinning with indecision, and consequently we've gone through two architects because I don't know what I want. Tom thinks I'm too picky. I think I'm going crazy. All I know is I want it to be perfect, so now I have to figure out what "perfect" means for me.

Unlike my nesting conundrum, the house wren isn't fussy at all when it comes to picking out a home.

The house wren is a small brown bird with a cocky tail that sticks straight up and a cocky attitude to match. The male wren arrives first in the spring. Unlike other songbirds that wait until the females arrive to start building nests, the male scouts out various locations and gets several "starter" nests underway. He knows she'll want to look a few over. Then, a few weeks later, his bride comes twittering into town and he gives her the grand tour of their real-estate options. Eventually she picks one. She then proceeds to throw out most of his sticks and add some of her own. Now she is content to call it home. But you'd be surprised at her definition of a suitable dwelling.

The funny thing about house-wren nests is where you find them. She is probably one of the most adaptable nesters in the songbird world. These wrens have been known to nest in the most amazing places: in shoes and boots, the pocket of pants on a clothesline, flowerpots, discarded tin cans, hanging plants, just about anywhere you can imagine. My neighbor Leslie had one build a nest in the decorative wreath on her front door. If you don't want your laundry or other personal items taken over as nesting spots, it would be smart to provide a home for the wren. And you do want them near your home because they have a beautiful warbling song and their favorite diet is all the destructive insects and bad bugs that are eating up your garden.

I think the best nesting box for a house wren is a free-swinging round cavity—like a hollowed-out gourd. Audubon Workshop has a fantastic catalog of all the nest boxes and birdseed you could want.[1] House wrens seem to prefer a free-swinging nest box to a standard, solid-mounted one. This is important to note because some researchers have discovered that wrens will take over most nest boxes in an area and discourage bluebirds, so if you're also trying to attract bluebirds, a free-swinging nest box for the wrens will free up the solid-mounted ones for the bluebirds. Also, it's important to have a wren house *without* an outside perch. Sparrows have been known to perch there and fend off wrens, even though they can't fit inside the smaller hole for wrens.

Wrens like being near people, and you will love to listen to them. I always try to visit my parents in the spring because my mother has two wren houses on opposite sides

---

[1] 812-537-3583, *http://audubonworkshop.com.*

of her home. (Wrens are territorial.) Every morning I wake up to a singing contest between the one in the front of the house and the one in the back. It is the joyful bubbling song of a carefree life. Some Native Americans called the wren *o-ðu-na-mis-sug-uð-ða-we-shi*, meaning, *making a big noise for its size.* I love it that God gave the wren this sweet trilling melody when it's such a small brown nondescript bird. The beautiful goldfinch and dashing red cardinal can't sing anywhere near the ode to joy of the wren. The wren's happy song is evident no matter if he's nesting in a pocket on the clothesline, an old boot, or a bona fide nesting box. His perpetually jaunty attitude is a wonderful example of sweet contentment. He is happy anywhere.

How completely different from what most of us experience. Most of us are focused on some target out there, further along in our lives, instead of enjoying and being content in the here and now. I have a friend who has a gorgeous home in the tropics. However, he is never content with it. Although he's redone several rooms, has all new furniture and a completely new wing, he's always thinking of some other area to improve or redecorate. (Trust me, the home is a showplace as it is.) How sad that he wastes his energy in this impossible goal of the perfect home. How sad that I frequently try to emulate him in my quest as well!

In contrast, I read in Philip Yancey's book *Soul Survivor* about the famous physician Paul Brand and what it was like growing up in a small home in India. Dr. Brand had lived in a modest handmade house his father built in India. He had also lived in England and America with all the accoutrements that those wealthy societies possess. The excess of the West made him uncomfortable. Yancey writes:

> Brand was still adjusting to life in the United States. He worried about the impact of television and the popular music culture on his children. Everyday luxuries made him nervous, and he longed for the simple life close to the soil in village India. When I talked him into going to a restaurant in the evening, he could hardly stand watching the waste of food scraped uneaten off diners' plates. He knew presidents, kings, and many famous people, but he rarely mentioned them, preferring instead to reminisce about individual leprosy patients. . . . Humility and gratitude flowed from him naturally, and in our time together I sensed a desperate lack of these qualities in myself.[2]

Obviously, Dr. Brand's sense of self-fulfillment wasn't based on the lifestyle we usually associate with famous physicians and all their perks. He shunned the designer home, the vacation homes, fancy cars, big-name people, dinners

---

[2]Philip Yancey, *Soul Survivor* (New York: Doubleday, 2001).

out, and yet he had abounding contentment, gratitude, and joy. I've seen this truth over and over again: wealth or achievement does not lead to happiness and contentment.

Tom and I have an extremely wealthy friend who has taken us on luxurious trips to Europe and to many beautiful restaurants. She has homes all over the world. She is also one of the most tortured, miserable people we know. She is constantly chasing after what she doesn't have. She is never content.

In contrast, Tom's parents as pastors of a small church have never had a secure fixed income but have spent their entire lives serving others through their church. They constantly have their home open to entertain people. Some are lonely and confused, some are old friends. They have never lacked food or shelter. They have far more meaning and contentment in their lives than anyone else we know, wealthy or not.

This Scripture sums up my point: "But godliness with contentment is great gain. For we brought nothing into the world, and we can take nothing out of it. But if we have food and clothing, we will be content with that. People who want to get rich fall into temptation and a trap and into many foolish and harmful desires that plunge men into ruin and destruction" (1 Timothy 6:6–9).

While listening to a radio show a couple of months ago, I heard the presenter talk about lifestyle expectations in the United States. He said we experience rampant discontent and frustration because we expect so much. We expect to start out with all the things it took our parents decades to achieve. We expect to have the lifestyle we see on TV or in magazines. We think it's our God-given right to own a home and a car. In contrast, he talked about the famous physicist Stephen Hawking. Confined for many years to a wheelchair because of debilitating Lou Gehrig's disease, Hawking had a different view. He said that when your expectations grind down to zero, just the simple act of looking out a window and pondering a tree can fill you with immense gratitude.

While I'm busily focused on building the perfect home, I find it easy to get wrapped up in what my *greeds* are, not my needs. What's far more important than the style and kinds of materials I choose is the personality and attitude I develop in the process. Will I urge my husband to take out loans and spend more than we can afford in order to match some magazine picture I have? (I have hundreds.) Will I demand that my home or our lifestyle live up to some expectation I have buried in my heart? Or will I be like the wren, content to define *home* in a variety of forms and sing a joyful song?

Never mind wood versus steel or tile versus granite; when I think about it, my attitude might be the most important building material of all. The foundation is up to me.

~ Mourning Dove ~

Softly, through the gauzy curtain of slumber, I could hear birds twittering over the humming fan in my bedroom. Occasionally the whine of a distant ski boat could be heard from the lake across the street. The humidity seemed to steam off the windowsills as the sun rose and began to simmer the cracked wooden ledges.

My mother would creep in and pretend to be astonished that I could still be asleep on such a warm, gorgeous morning. She'd open up the rolling window shades and sing, "A birdie with a yellow bill hopped upon my window sill, cocked his shiny eye and said, 'Ain't you awake, you sleepy head?' "[1] I'd stretch, wonder if my friends were already out

---

[1]Paraphrase of "Time to Rise," Robert Louis Stevenson.

water-skiing, and think about breakfast.

Stepping outside to do my chores
(clean out the birdbath and pull dan-
delions), I would hear the coo of a bird. I
asked my mother, who knew all the bird-
songs in our area, which bird it was. What she actually
said, versus how I interpreted it, made all the difference in
my perception of that particular bird.

What I heard her say was, "That's a morning dove." *How
sweet!* I thought. A dove to greet you in the morning. A dove
to announce it's another beautiful day brimming with opportunities and adventures. I thought their plump little bodies
were cute. I thought it was neat the way they fed their young
"pigeon milk," a white milklike liquid the parents regurgi-
tated. I thought about how brides on their wedding day
often let doves loose to celebrate, and I marveled at how perfectly the morning dove would fit that occasion.

So for a long time, whenever I heard the coo of mourning
doves, *coo-ahh, coo, coo, coooo*, I would be charmed, associating
it with happy things and fresh dewy mornings full of potential.

Years later, I was dismayed to find out that my softly cooing birds in their taupe gray morning suits weren't greeting
the day with soft "good mornings." They weren't *morning*
doves at all. They were *mourning* doves. A whole world of
difference. Now when I heard their cooing I thought of

plaintive calls and mournful crying at funerals. I thought it was depressing. I didn't want to hear them anymore. I imagined their mournful coos in the morning as messages of misfortunes to come.

But what really sealed my disillusionment of mourning doves was when I discovered their nesting habits. Our backyard had a scrubby forested area with some dense shrubs. In one of these I found a sloppily made nest. Most of it was lying on the ground in tatters with some eggs smashed. I went running inside to tell my mother.

"This is awful!" I cried to her. "Some cat or animal got into this nest and destroyed it. The poor birds!" My mother came outside to look at the nest with me. "It must have been the wind last night," she said. "It wasn't a very strong wind, but that's a mourning dove nest and they make them so loose and sloppy that they fall apart easily."

"You mean just *this* one made a sloppy nest?" I asked.

"No," she said, "they *all* make nests like this. That's just the way it is."

That's just the way it is? That wasn't good enough for me. And it was the final twig. Not only did they fail to greet the sunrise with welcoming coos, but they were the official bird of mourning. Plus, they were so stupid that they couldn't even build a nest right so as to keep their future family safe. They didn't live up to what I thought they were and my idea of what a proper songbird should be: cheerfully raising young in secure nests and greeting each morning with a joyful noise. I was disappointed and disgusted with mourning doves. I decided to avoid them in the future.

The doves hadn't changed at all; my perception of who they were and how they were supposed to act had been altered and I didn't like it. I preferred my time of mistaken identity instead of the reality.

I went through the same issue of mistaken identity in my perception of God as well.

Many believers are attracted to the fold because of the oft-quoted promise, "God has something good in store for you." This is backed up by the verse, " 'For I know the plans I have for you,' declares the Lord, 'plans to prosper you and not to harm you, plans to give you hope and a future' " (Jeremiah 29:11). While this verse is true, sometimes it gets twisted to suit our desires. In this day when self-fulfillment and personal happiness are seen as our God-given birthright, a results-oriented God is too good to pass up. But what do we do when this Mr. Good-Times God doesn't do what we expect Him to?

God didn't turn out to be who I wanted Him to be. I wanted a God that helped me out of crises, cured me when I was sick, generally answered prayers favorably (or at least made known His opinion and didn't leave me in the dark). I wanted a God who kept my family safe and healthy, got me job opportunities, and kept me from the fires of hell for eternity. I wanted Him to be useful, and I thought His conditions were fair. His rules weren't too hard to follow.

Treat others the way you would like to be treated. Forgive others — even your enemies — and pray often. What was so tough? What's not to like?

Then I grew up. And who I thought God was took a beating. He didn't perform the way I thought He was supposed to. He let horrible things happen to people I loved. He let illness, death, and broken hearts happen. In the world around me children were starving, the nasty were getting richer, people were getting murdered, mothers were getting breast cancer, and nice guys were finishing last. I didn't like this new God. Although He wasn't new at all. He had never changed. What needed to change were my expectations and mistaken ideas of who God was.

Minister and writer Dr. R. T. Kendall says that most believers will hit the "betrayal barrier" at some point in their Christian life. This will happen when they go through a period of heartache, loss, and a sense of God's abandonment. Their situation doesn't make sense and it's unfair.

In my earlier book *Gardening Mercies*, I talked about a difficult time when I was grieving, depressed, and quite angry with God. My prayers and fasting did no good as far as I could see, and worst of all, it didn't make sense. This wasn't the kind of God I signed up for.

Fortunately, the Bible shows that I'm not the only one who struggles with expectations over how God should act. I always smile with recognition when I read of John the Baptist's question from prison. John had been faithful, living an exemplary life, preparing the way for "one who is greater," and pointing people toward Jesus. He ended up in prison and instructed one of his followers to ask Jesus, "Are you the one who was to come, or should we expect someone else?" (Matthew 11:3). Under the circumstances, life didn't make sense to John so he doubted Jesus' deity and authority.

The disciples faced this hurdle of mistaken identity as well. They thought Jesus came to overthrow the Roman government and be their earthly king. They were jostling over who would sit on his right or his left in the coming kingdom. After he was arrested and appeared to be power-less—not the king they had imagined Him to be—Peter said in effect, "Am I associated with him? No way."

I believe that many people who have summarily rejected the Christian faith suffer from disillusionment and dashed expectations as well. They look at the judgmental and un-loving people who call themselves Christians and decide, "Forget it. You were supposed to love me, to feed me, to come alongside of me and hug me—not stand back and tell me how to live. If that's who your Jesus is, you can have Him."

The root of this disillusionment with God is that our sit-uations don't make sense. We can't understand what He is doing. The Bible says that God is love, but the things that happen to us don't seem very loving. James Dobson, in his book *When God Doesn't Make Sense,* describes this process of shattered expectations.

It is the absence of meaning that make their situation so intolerable. . . . It is not uncommon to hear a confused Christian express great agitation, anger, or even blasphemy. This confused individual is like a little girl being told by her divorced father that he will come to see her. When Daddy fails to show up, she suffers far more than if he had never offered to come.

The key word here is expectations. They set us up for disillusionment. There is no greater distress in human experience than to build one's entire way of life on a certain theological understanding, and then have it collapse at a time of unusual stress and pain.[2]

In this day and age we can predict weather patterns and storms. We can identify disease hidden deep within our mysterious organs, and we have almost finished unraveling our genetic code — God's blueprint of our human bodies. We believe that with enough perseverance and technology we can figure everything out. It doesn't sit well with us to hear "lean not on your own understanding" (Proverbs 3:5).

But time and time again, that's the message God gives us through His Word. Accepting the fact that with God there will always be some mystery also happens to be the key to jumping over the betrayal barrier. We want answers and explanations; God wants relationship and trust.

Trust in what? That things will get better? No, because

---

[2]James Dobson, *When God Doesn't Make Sense* (Wheaton, Ill.: Tyndale House Publishers, Inc., 1993).

oftentimes our situations (like John the Baptist, who was beheaded) become worse. But we *can* trust that He knows what He's doing. He loves us and He promises to take the miserable circumstances of our lives and use them for good.

He took the sordid life of a prostitute who gratefully washed His feet and made it into an exemplary illustration that would stand for eternity. He changed a murdering, judgmental know-it-all named Saul into a powerful instrument of reconciliation and grace. He transformed an undisciplined, rash traitor named Peter into a brave and powerful witness of His love. Like the negative bumper sticker that says, "Life sucks and then you die," Jesus assures us that "in this world you will have trouble" (John 16:33). But He can take our painful situations and use them in astonishing ways if we will let go of our expectations and demands to understand Him on our own terms.

I was listening to the radio one day and was struck by a young woman's lack of a sense of entitlement. She was the devoted Christian mother of a toddler when she inexplicably went blind. Then several months later her husband died of a brain tumor. Her response was, "I never asked, 'why me?' I thought, 'Why *not* me? I'm no better than anyone else.'" This attitude, I realized, was completely foreign to me. I was complaining and demanding that God ought not to treat me this way. I wanted Him to explain himself to me. Even though this woman was blind, she could see our proper standing before God much clearer than I could.

Madame Jeanne Guyon said, "If knowing answers to life's questions is absolutely necessary to you, then forget the journey. You will never make it, for this is a journey of unknowables—of unanswered questions, enigmas, incomprehensibles, and most of all, things unfair."[3]

The sufferings of Job are renowned. He went through the loss of everything he owned, his health, and his family, save for his wife, who encouraged him to "curse God and die." He didn't curse God, but he did complain. He did ask, as we all do, *Why me? Why this?*

Philip Yancey writes about God's answer to Job, "To the problem of pain itself, however, God gave no direct answer, only this challenge to Job: If I, as Creator, have produced such a marvelous world as this, which you can plainly observe, can you not trust me with those areas you cannot comprehend?"[4]

Instead of trying to explain to Job the what and why of how He operates in this world, God pointed to His creation. God asks, "Who is this that darkens my counsel with words without knowledge? Brace yourself like a man; I will ques-

---

[3]Jeanne Guyon, *Spiritual Torrents* (Jacksonville, FL: Seed Sowers, Revised edition 1989).
[4]Philip Yancey, *Reaching for the Invisible God* (Grand Rapids, Mich.: Zondervan Publishing House, 2000).

tion you, and you shall answer me. Where were you when I laid the earth's foundation? Tell me, if you understand. . . . Can you bring forth the constellations in their seasons. . . ? Do you know the laws of the heavens?" (Job 38: 2–4, 32–33).

There is a joke about how scientists got together with God and said, "We understand how everything came into being and with our technology we can create just as you can." So they set out to re-create man from the dust of the earth. The scientists bent down and scooped up some dust. God said, "Wait a minute, go make your own dust."

One of my husband's good friends is the former chief scientist for Xerox, John Seely Brown. John has written books, is widely quoted, and is known as possessing an amazing and gifted mind. Tom has a science background in physics. When those two get together and start talking about things in the universe (like quantum physics, qualitative physics, string theory, and cognitive science), my head begins to spin. Most of the time, I can barely pick up the threads of what they are talking about. The things I *am* able to slightly comprehend are so huge that it feels like the seams in my brain are creaking and stretching—just about to snap. I can't speak most of their language, even when it's English. They talk about things far above what most people in the world can comprehend. This scenario reminds me of something I heard Hank Hanegraaff say about God explaining himself to us: "It's like trying to explain the universe to a small-necked clam."

We want—or even demand—to know how God works. *He* wants us to face who He is. He created us. He wants us to drop our attitudes and suppositions about Him.

We live in a world that is unfair, where we "will have trouble," where life is tough. If the disciples had to suffer and the Son of God had to suffer, who are we to think we should be exempt? We suffer from a case of mistaken identity when we think God exists just to make our lives smoother. Our tough times may be the ticket to our greatest joy—a deeper relationship with the One who made us, being fully known and fully aware of how deeply we are loved.

Despite my times of pounding on God's chest and my frustration over things not lining up with my expectations, I am attracted to Him because He allows me this freedom. I like a God who sticks by me—even when I'm full of doubts and irritated. Jacob was a schemer and tried to bargain with God. He wanted life on his own terms. God looked past all that and saw Jacob's heart and stuck with him throughout his struggles.

I would expect God to get disgusted with my wandering heart, my predilection to sin, my whining for answers. I am surprised by His unconditional love and gift of second chances. I've found that He's the God of the fat chance, the slim chance, and the last chance. I'm delighted that God isn't at all what I expected.

Mourning doves aren't any less lovely in sound or form just because I was mistaken about who they are. And God isn't any less powerful, right, or loving when I am mistaken about who He is.

After I let go of my expectations, I came to appreciate the mourning dove's gentle behavior and gentle cooing. I view their mournful song as a clarion call to remind me life is short, my demise is certain, and to make the most of today.

I'm still learning to shed a lot of my expectations about who God is, and I suspect it's a lifelong process. Sometimes when I'm outdoors and I see something breathtakingly beautiful and sublime, I want to hop into His lap, give Him a big hug, and tell Him, "Thank you!" Other times when I see tragedies that don't make sense, I wonder if He's sleeping on the job or uncaring. But I'll never stop being fascinated by, intrigued by, and alternating between love, fear, and anxiety about who He is and what He's doing with my life. The only thing I can expect from this relationship is that it will be full of ups and downs, joys and disappointments, and all in my best interests. First Corinthians 2:9 says that "no eye has seen, no ear has heard, no mind has conceived what God has prepared for those who love him." That I can look forward to with great expectation.

~ *Robin* ~

Spring is a frustrating time in the Midwest. Just when daffodil leaves were poking above the hard earth and the crocuses were croaking through bits of snow and spring seemed just around the corner, we would get a huge dump of snow. And even when the snow ultimately *was* on its way out the door, it would leave in an ugly, rebellious way. When the snow first arrived, it came with grace and beauty, dusting everything with dainty powdered sugar. When it started to dissipate, it did so in a sullen manner, leaving slumpy banks blackened by cars and slushy gray heaps everywhere. Like a guest who'd overstayed her welcome, winter seemed to hang around forever. I couldn't wait for it to finally *leave*. I longed for the reality of spring.

That's why I understood my friend Janet's assessment of

the robin. When I asked her why she liked the robin she said, "After living in the Midwest for many years, where the winters seemed to go on and on *forever* with sub-zero temperatures, ice storms, and surprise March snowstorms, I'd have to say the robin is my favorite. When you see the robin, you finally can have hope that spring is truly here."

I have a soft spot in my heart for robins for the very same reason. Although they are commonly seen hopping around lawns and pulling up worms throughout North America, it was always a thrill when my mother's voice would ring out, "Look! There's a robin in the yard today!" With its cheery orange-red breast, it was the sign that although there may still have been some snowdrifts piled high, spring was officially on its way. The robin was proof positive because they are usually the first birds to arrive.

In America we are obsessed about being first. We remember who won the gold medal in the Olympics, but we can't quite name the silver or bronze medalists. Instead of being thrilled that they made it to the Super Bowl or the World Series, the team that doesn't win calls itself the loser. (Aren't the losers the ones who didn't make it to the top event at all or were last in their division?) We immortalize the words of Vince Lombardi: "Winning isn't everything; it's the *only* thing."

In my youth I would get so frustrated when, after a swimming race, the only question some people would ask was, "Did you win?" Not, "Did you try your hardest?" or, "Did you get a personal best time?" It was always whether or not I *won*. If I didn't win but tried my hardest or set a school record, I still felt like it wasn't enough, that I didn't measure up. To this day I don't revel in the fact that I achieved NCAA Division I All-American status; I feel like a phony because I only *qualified* for that label by finishing in the top sixteen relay teams at the national meet — I didn't *win*. I could also go on about how it wasn't even an individual event but a *relay* with others. . . . You get the picture. Instead of rejoicing over how far I'd come, I focused on what I didn't achieve and the fact that I wasn't first.

I didn't see this attitude when I lived in Australia for a couple of years. There, people valued the effort, the fact that you "had a go at it." I heard parents and friends saying "Good job!" to kids who put their hearts into it — instead of screaming at the coaches or other parents like the Little League and hockey parents we see in the news today. In that culture I saw it was more important to participate in sports than to be satisfied only with winning. When it comes to life in general, and in particular our spiritual paths, we need to have this attitude too.

Unfortunately, our tendency is to rush into lots of religious activities in order to stack up "points" with God. We have the misguided notion that there is some sort of hierarchic game within His church that we can win.

I have an acquaintance who whenever asked "How are things going?" responds with an impressive list of saintly accomplishments. "Well, I've been *mentoring* a lot of women at church," she gushes, "and *leading* several prayer groups *and* teaching Sunday school." Even though I know she probably exaggerates the truth to make herself look good, after listening to her, I feel inferior. I feel like God probably approves of her more than of me. I start to compare my list to hers. Due to my competitive nature, I want to be first in the God-accomplishment race and I want to kick her holier-than-thou shins.

While humans may elevate certain positions above others, to God "all have sinned and fall short of [His] glory" (Romans 3:23). Or as the old saying goes, "The ground is level at the foot of the cross." He doesn't love St. Peter or Mother Teresa any more than He loves the murderer who confesses faith in Christ before he dies. Our job is to respond with who we are and what we have to what He has called us to. Who *are* we in His eyes? What *has* He called us to? To be *children of God* (Romans 8:16), *friends of Christ* (John 15:15), and *loved and chosen by God* (1 Thessalonians 1:4). These aren't things we can run a race to win or claw our way to the top for. We are first in God's heart whether we are the best or worst at running races, evangelizing, or changing diapers. Our position is not based on performance.

If the robin were human, she'd probably think, "I'm so well loved because I produce those famous blue eggs." Or,

"I make the best mud-and-stick nests." And yes, those are neat things about the robin. But that's not why I appreciate robins. I'm grateful for their presence because they give me hope. Hope that there is a genuine, lasting thaw just around the corner. Hope that the winter's death grip won't hold on forever.

God wants us to understand that He doesn't love us based on what we can do for Him (which is laughable when you think about it—what can we possibly do for the Creator of the universe that He can't do for himself?). He loves us just because we *are*. And this is a good thing when you think about how many times we screw up in a single day.

I'm so thankful for the examples of everyday schmucks in the Bible. The things we think are important—position, intelligence, money, education, and beauty—don't factor in when God chooses people to get close to or work with. Moses was a murderer, but God used him to rescue a nation from slavery. Rahab was a prostitute, but God used

her to help Joshua capture Jericho. Solomon had a gluttonous libido and he ignored God's warning on foreign women, but God blessed him with extraordinary wisdom. Paul was a murderer of Christians, but God used him to evangelize nations and write Scripture. Peter was an impetuous trai-tor, but God used him to spread the Gospel to nations, write Scripture, and establish the church.

When the prophet Samuel was told to pick out the next king of Israel from a lineup of accomplished and handsome brothers, God told him not to be impressed with their stature or looks because "the Lord does not look at the things man looks at. Man looks at the outward appearance, but the Lord looks at the heart" (1 Samuel 16:7). God told Samuel that the simple shepherd boy David was the one he wanted. In fact, despite the fact that He knew David would later go on to commit adultery and murder, God said David was "a man after his own heart" (1 Samuel 13:14, Acts 13:22). In light of what David did, I find this fact stunning. Obviously, it means a great deal to God to have a man or woman "after his own heart" but what does that look like?

First of all, it's about putting God first in all areas of our lives. In David's psalms we see him crying out to God in all kinds of situations—running for his life, angry at his enemies, wondering if God had abandoned him or didn't love him anymore. David turned to God first with all his concerns, in praise and petition. God wants to be first in every area of our lives. He wants us to run to Him first with our concerns and fears, even before we pick up the phone and call our friends. He wants us to care more about what He thinks than our parents, friends, or the neighbors next door think. Therapists' offices are full of people who are wasting their lives trying to please those people—some of whom are dead—to no avail. Parenting problems, travel, business decisions—all are important to Him. No sin, addiction, or lust for material gain is too nasty for Him to hear about.

The Bible demonstrates that He is always willing to hear from us about everything. "Cast all your anxiety on him because he cares for you" (1 Peter 5:7) and "Come to me, all you who are weary and burdened, and I will give you rest" (Matthew 11:28). What part of *all* don't we understand? Instead, we shrink back. We act as if this reads, "Come to me, all who have your act together, who do many good works and appear outwardly perfect. Then I will delight to hear from you."

Recently, the Barna Institute did a survey as to why evangelical Christians don't share their faith more. The answer wasn't that they felt they didn't know enough. The answer wasn't that they were self-conscious or embarrassed. The answer was that they didn't feel their lives were a good enough example, so who were they to talk about the right path to follow? Although I understand this attitude (and have felt that way myself), it is a wrong assumption. We think we have to be perfect to talk about a perfect God. As God demonstrated with Moses, Rahab, David, Solomon, Paul, and Peter, He regularly uses imperfect humans to display and communicate who He is. It's all about sharing God's love from a humble position, not from a false front of perfection.

Anne Lamott expressed this perfectly for me in her book *Traveling Mercies*. She was on a plane sitting next to someone who asked her if she was a Christian. She responded, "Yes, I am." But then she thought, "I'm just a bad Christian. A bad born-again Christian. And certainly, like the apostle Peter, I am capable of denying it, of presenting myself as a sort of leftist liberation-theology enthusiast and maybe sort of a vaguely Jesusy bon vivant."[1] If we're honest with ourselves, most of us feel this way at times.

God knows we're fickle, wavering, semi-believing phonies much of the time. And He wants us anyway. As we buy a used car with a couple of dents and badly worn brakes, He takes us "as is." We have to constantly remind ourselves that we have nothing to offer so we can stop pretending that we do. Martin Luther said, "God creates out of nothing. Therefore until a man is nothing, God can make nothing out of him." And Paul said, "I know that nothing good lives in me, that is, in my sinful nature. For I have the desire to do what is good, but I cannot  carry it out" (Romans 7:18). The only reason we have any affection or love for God is because He loved us first in the midst of our sins and brokenness. "We love because He first loved us" (1 John 4:19). What we *can* offer Him is our total

---

[1]Anne Lamott, *Traveling Mercies* (New York: Pantheon Books, 1999), 61.

selves; our wounded hearts, abused bodies, and traitorous minds He will not despise.

We too, like David, can be men and women "after God's own heart" despite our past mistakes and current failings. All we need to do is admit we are stumbling phonies who desperately need His help every day and turn to Him first. Then we can share our faith with others with credibility. Like the woman at the well who had had five husbands, we can tell others, "I don't have it all together, but I can definitely point you to the One who does!" It's not about us; it's about Him.

When I see how God used the broken lives of Moses, David, and Peter, it gives me hope. Hope that I don't have to have it all together. Hope that He can do something beautiful and meaningful with my life. Like the robin that is the first to arrive with the promise of spring, when we put God first, we can have the promise of spring in our lives. No matter how frozen, dead, and dormant our hearts, He can cause new life to spring up within us. And that's a first-place finish worth aiming for.

~ Cedar Waxwing ~

I wouldn't trade my office window view for anything in the world. Just to the left of my computer monitor is a nearly six-foot-wide picture window. It overlooks our backyard, which is a symphony of flora and fauna. Right now in March there are pink and white cyclamen everywhere, a few roses are budding out, the purple and white wisterias are starting to bloom, and the fountain is happily babbling away. The hummingbird feeder is about twelve feet from my window, the bees are hovering over the orange blossoms nearby, and a few birds are darting around with nesting material in their beaks. It's my little slice of paradise. So I was pretty surprised the other morning to see this normally quiet, peaceful haven teeming with what seemed like hundreds of birds.

All the trees and rosebushes appeared to be moving and

shaking, there were so many birds in them. *What is going on?* I wondered. Grabbing my miniature binoculars I took a closer look. Cedar waxwings! I hadn't seen a group like this since I left the Midwest years ago.

Cedar waxwings are cinnamon-brown birds with glamorous touches. Instead of a plain rounded head, they have a sleek crest on top, followed by an elegant, dramatic black mask across their eyes (think masquerade party). Their brown coloring gives way to a soft yellow on the belly. The tip of the tail has a yellow band, which all waxwings have. And the tips of the secondary feathers on their wings are red. It's this red tip that gives them their name. The red material has a waxy consistency and is secreted from the shafts of their secondary feathers. It's not known for certain what the function is of these red tips, but it might serve as a breeding signal, because it doesn't appear until their second year. If you watch them long enough, you might observe their charming feeding habit. They love berries, and sometimes they can be seen passing a berry from bird to bird until one of them finally takes it.

To attract cedar waxwings you need trees and shrubs that produce berries. They enjoy pyracantha, cotoneaster, mountain ash, juniper, and hawthorns. I do have berry-producing bushes, but I also think they flock here because I have a lot of water in my yard. Bird enthusiasts I've met on the Internet say they've had large flocks around their birdbaths and fountains. You'll never have a problem sighting one cedar waxwing, because they travel in flocks of about fifty, always keeping company with loads of their friends. I wonder if the person who penned "Birds of a feather flock together" wrote it about cedar waxwings.

When I was fresh out of college and attending a new church, I fell in with a large sociable crowd of friends. This was important because I was new to the area and didn't know many people. It was a great feeling to be with others who shared the same interests and beliefs. Unfortunately, it was too insular. This was the only group I socialized with. After a while we all looked the same, acted the same, and thought the same. We weren't interested in reaching out to the hurting and disadvantaged around us. We were interested in having fun and being right. In this church, despite its solid teaching (and I got a great foundation there), being doctrinally right was oftentimes more important than being loving.

One of my friends, I'll call her Jennifer, started seeing someone who was from a different faith. That wasn't the only thing different about him. He treated her differently than the Christian guys in our group did. He wasn't concerned that she wasn't model-thin or that she didn't have a

serious career or that she couldn't debate the merits of Cal-
vinism versus Arminian theology. He loved her infectious
laugh, her sense of humor and adventurous spirit. Soon,
Jennifer fell madly in love with him and spent a great deal
of time with him and his parents. This made her the source
of much concern (that's a Christian euphemism for *gossip*)
among our group.

We tried to reason with her, shame her, and do everything we could to get her to see the error of her ways. The
one thing we *didn't* do, what Jesus commanded us to do, was
communicate to her our unconditional friendship and love
no matter what her behavior. So, since we couldn't change
her, we simply reasoned she wasn't serious about her faith in
God and clucked our collective tongues.

Months later, brokenhearted, Jennifer called it off and
picked up the pieces. She returned to our fellowship and
Bible study. One assiduous young man greeted her with
veiled accusation and condemnation: "Well, Jennifer, where
have *you* been?" I wanted to applaud her answer. She said,
"On the other side of hell. Where were *you*?"

When my friend Bill's wife deserted him and left him
with several children to raise by himself, many of his Christian friends deserted too. It was his non-Christian friends
who took him Christmas caroling to shut-ins in nursing
homes. It was his non-Christian friends who checked in on
him, listened to him, and included him in their social activities. Maybe the church friends thought divorce was catch-

ing, or they secretly blamed him or thought God was punishing him for some heinous deed. His Christian counselor assessed this behavior succinctly: "Unfortunately, Christians often shoot their wounded."

Galatians 6:1–3 reads, "Brothers, if someone is caught in a sin, you who are spiritual should restore him gently. But watch yourself, or you also may be tempted. Carry each other's burdens, and in this way you will fulfill the law of Christ. If anyone thinks he is something when he is nothing, he deceives himself." I like the way *The Message*, by Eugene Peterson, paraphrases this. "Live creatively, friends. If someone falls into sin, forgivingly restore him, saving your critical comments for yourself. *You* might be needing forgiveness before the day's out. Stoop down and reach out to those who are oppressed. Share their burdens, and so complete Christ's law. If you think you are too good for that, you are badly deceived."

In both versions, the word *restore* is used. My thesaurus tells me that renew, repair, reinstate, and reestablish are synonyms for restore. It's so much easier to point out flaws than to "stoop down" and do the hard work of coming alongside and helping. Author Brennan Manning describes a time when he was an alcoholic priest. It got so bad he was living in the gutter. The friend who helped pull him out of this miserable state didn't come and speak to him about what he should do, where he went wrong, or the twelve steps of AA. His friend simply sat there in silence and love, day after day.

This act of love and kindness is what moved Brennan. Eventually he found his way back to wholeness and was restored.

I frequently make the mistake of thinking that I need to tell people what to do with their lives, or at least give them my opinion. It's as if I believe I'll receive demerits when I reach heaven because I didn't tell everyone where they were missing the mark. (This behavior is not a big hit with my husband.) Concerned about my judgmental tendencies, I asked Tom once how he thought we—and me in particular—could do a better job of living our faith. He said (partially quoting a comedian), "I think Christians need to shut their big yappers and just *love* people!"

This is not unfamiliar to me. My girlfriend Daniela, who lives in Australia, told me once, "My only job is to *love*. No matter what shape, form, method, and time." Like the cedar waxwing with his red identifying mark, maybe it's time I make *love* the identifying mark of my Christian faith. Maybe when we join the flock on Sunday mornings we need to dust off that song and sing, "They will know we are Christians by our love."

~ *Meadowlark* ~

Our boots crunched and squished in the muddy gravel as we walked. On either side of us, bright orange poppies were waking up to the rising sun. Five hundred feet below us, traces of fog licked up the mountainside, embracing the trees and blotting out their shapes. Wisps of the fog's dewy tendrils occasionally drifted by as we walked on the dirt path. Stellar jays scolded us with raspy caws in the pine trees above us. The air was bracing, piney, clean, and straight off the Pacific Ocean, which lay before us in a panoramic 180-degree view. Over to the east, the sun was peeking over the ridges, warming the hills and pushing back the fog in a battle for ownership rights on the land.

It was a gorgeous morning on the mountain where we hope to move to someday.

Normally, such an extravagance of scenic splendor would overwhelm me, taking my breath away. Sometimes I'm so astonished by the tenderness and vulnerability of our fragile environment that I feel almost sad. But I was oblivious to all this beauty. Well, maybe not oblivious, but I certainly wasn't appreciating it. My mind was full of worries. I was worrying about our current lease. Should we sign up for another year of exorbitant rent, or should we move? I was worrying about Tom's new job. Was he happy? Did we make the right choice? Could we adjust to the lower salary? I was worried about the building plans. I didn't know how to assess whether I would like living in the layouts that were presented to me. I was terrified of making a mistake I would have to live with the rest of my life. I was worrying about how to become educated in passive solar systems and green building materials. I was worried about building costs. I was worried about a relative's chronic disease. Would he end up in a wheelchair? Should we put ramps in our plans? My mind was preoccupied with the clamor of festering worries that morning.

That is, until I heard the singing. Tom and I rounded a bend in the path and were greeted by the most unearthly flute song. We stopped abruptly in wonder. The clatter and voices in my head silenced as I focused in on the source. The song lifted and floated through the early morning stillness. It rose and fell in undulating, watery notes that seemed to pour forth from a source of pure bubbling joy.

On a boulder not twenty feet from us sat a bird, tilting its head back and offering up his exaltation to the day's beginning. Another bird, a small distance away, answered back with his own ode to joy.

The beauty of it all stunned us. The view, the song, the otherworldliness of the scene snapped us out of our thoughts and conversation and into a moment of contemplative peace. It was as if one moment we were in the midst of the roaring turbulence of Niagara Falls and the next, in dead silence broken only by a flute.

I thought I knew what the bird was, but the sun was in my eyes and I wasn't sure. If it *was* what I thought, then God had just given me an incredible gift. Days later I questioned our neighbor.

"I saw this bird," I said with hesitation. "I think it had a yellow front and mottled back. Could it be—have you ever seen . . . *meadowlarks* around here?"

"Yes, that was a western meadowlark," he said. "There are a lot of them over on your parcel."

Lots of them on our parcel? I felt like weeping in gratitude.

The last time I had heard a meadowlark was when I was twelve years old on a camping trip. There were fields all around us and I remember hearing a bird singing a gorgeous song. It was so striking several of us girls wondered what it was. Our camp counselor told us it was a meadowlark, and I thought I would never forget that sound.

Decades later I *did* forget the sound, but I remembered the bird. I remembered that the meadowlark has a lilting, flute-like song unlike any other. To hear it soaring over the fresh new morning, to think of living up on that mountain next to the wonder and waking daily to such a gift is like a kiss from God.

There's a reason I hadn't heard the meadowlark for so many years. They like *meadows*. Meaning large, open fields of unmown grasses that you usually find in more rural settings. This is becoming rarer these days as more and more grasslands are being turned into suburbs and shopping malls. (Now you have an excuse not to mow every blessed inch of your property.) Meadowlarks build their nests on the ground, so unleashed pets[1] are a significant threat. The meadowlark nest is so well hidden that you'd probably step on it before you realized it's there. They build their nests with grasses in depressions in the ground and then heap more grasses and sticks over the top to create a cavelike structure. While their nests may be difficult to detect, the meadowlark itself is not difficult to identify. Both the eastern and the western versions have a bright yellow chest and

[1] Check out *www.audubon.org/bird/cat/* for information on the Cats Indoors! Program. Contrary to popular belief, a bell on the domestic cat does not make it any safer for songbirds. Millions are killed each year, and ground-nesting birds are seriously threatened by cats outdoors. (Plus, cats live an average of less than five years when they roam freely outside, while indoor cats often live seventeen or more years.)

throat with a distinct black V-shape marking at the base of the throat. Their backs and wings are a mottled mixture with brown, black, and white markings (to help them blend in with the grasses). The Eastern meadowlark has a brighter yellow chest than its more subdued Western cousin does, but I'm thrilled to report that the Western version has the better song.

Before I heard the lyrical melody that morning, I was worrying about whether or not I really wanted to live on this property full time. I was worried it was too remote. I was worried I'd go crazy like those frontier women with nobody to talk to so they ended up muttering to the trees. Although I hate traffic noise, I was worried it was *too* quiet up there. Also, it was a new area for me and I didn't have any friends nearby. The heavenly aria of the meadowlark lifted me out of my minor worries and concerns and gave me new reverence for the opportunity to live amidst God's beauty. I was transported away from all my interior musings of "what if?" and my eyes were opened to a totally new perspective. My vision shifted from what I didn't have and what I might not get to the possibilities and glories of what I *did* and *could* have. That's what gratitude is supposed to do—widen our

vision, change our outlook, and reevaluate our circumstances.

Author André Dubus described my attitude when he said, "It is not hard to live through a day if you can live through a moment. What creates despair is the imagination, which pretends there is a future and insists on predicting millions of moments, thousands of days, and so drains you that you cannot live the moment at hand." Instead of enjoying the moment, I was projecting years into the future. In her enchanting book *Attitudes of Gratitude,* author M. J. Ryan says, "Gratitude brings you back to the present moment, to all that is working perfectly right now."[2] There is always a choice before us, to focus on what's missing and wrong with our lives or focus on what's right and good. Like spoiled children on Christmas morning, we tear through all the wonderful gifts we've been given and take for granted (I have friends, health, and work) and then whine and complain about what we don't have.

This attitude of gratefulness is not natural or easy for some of us. I'm kind of a curmudgeon by nature. Overly peppy motivational speakers and sales people make my skin crawl. Some friends suggest it's my Scandinavian background; others think it's my achievement-oriented upbringing. Tom thinks it's because of my years as an art director on photo shoots; my eye is trained to look for wrinkled clothing and stray hairs. I have to force myself from noticing what's wrong in a situation (doesn't my husband *see* the food stuck on the pan he's just washed?) and purposely focus on what's right and good (he washed the pan).

---

[2]M. J. Ryan, *Attitudes of Gratitude: How to Give and Receive Joy Every Day of Your Life* (York Beach, ME.: Conari Press, 1999).

If I were to name the opposite of gratitude I would say it's a sense of entitlement. This attitude says, *I ought to have this — in fact, I deserve it*, and leads to resentment and bitterness when our desires are thwarted. We think we deserve a certain lifestyle, a certain response from loved ones, acknowledgment for our accomplishments, and rewards for hard work. For years I struggled with this and still do sometimes. But I find life a lot sweeter and more joy filled when I concentrate on all the blessings I have that I don't deserve. Although most days I wake up with a stiff, aching back and twenty extra pounds that I can't seem to lose and a never-ending pile of things to work through, I *can* delight in other things. I've never had a bad hair day — I have gloriously thick hair. I'm married to a wonderful man who loves to cook and write me poetry. I haven't been successful in having children, but I'm thankful I have choices, like adoption. I'm learning to stop expecting my life to be a certain way and enjoy what *is*. Tom told me that he learned from his parents to have this attitude in life: whatever *is*, is *good*; the alternative is a dissatisfied, grumbling, and miserable outlook. C. S. Lewis said, "It seems to me that we often, almost sulkily, reject the good that God offers us because, at the moment, we expected some other good." And the wisdom from Proverbs 15:15 teaches us, "All the days of the oppressed are wretched, but the cheerful heart has a continual feast."

One of the surprise hit albums at the Grammy Awards

recently was the music from the movie *O Brother, Where Art Thou?* Maybe that's because it contains many homey, old-fashioned bluegrass tunes such as "Keep on the Sunny Side"—a song that speaks of an attitude adjustment that's rare in today's angst-ridden society. It seems foolish in this day of terrorism and worldwide problems to look on the sunny side of life, but God tells us it's the secret to peace, contentment, and a productive life. The apostle Paul (who had been shipwrecked, stoned, left for dead, and jailed and knew all about abuse and hard times) said, "Rejoice in the Lord always. I will say it again: Rejoice! Let your gentleness be evident to all. The Lord is near. Do not be anxious about anything, but in everything, by prayer and petition, with thanksgiving, present your requests to God. And the peace of God, which transcends all understanding, will guard your hearts and your minds in Christ Jesus" (Philippians 4:4–7).

Not only does it please God; gratitude does *us* good as we focus on the riches outside of us and not the clamor and worries in our heads. Sometimes, gratefulness is an act of the will. When life is tough and our plans are falling apart, gratefulness becomes a sacrifice when we're not feeling particularly thankful or worshipful. But it *is* possible.

Barbara Johnson has written several humor-filled books about circumstances that aren't so funny. One son was killed in Vietnam, another was killed by a truck on a freeway, and a third son cut off communication with the family when he embraced an alternative lifestyle. Now *that's* pain. But her books *Stick a Geranium in Your Hat and Be Happy* and *Splashes of Joy in the Cesspools of Life* are bestsellers. My friend Laura Jensen Walker wrote a hilarious book about her experience with breast cancer, *Thanks for the Mammogram*. When my father had cancer, my brother got divorced, and I failed for the fourth year in a row to get pregnant, Joan Rivers's book *Bouncing Back* helped me find my way out of the gloom—with a few hearty guffaws as well. While none of these experiences are in themselves funny, the writers did find moments of laughter and gratefulness in spite of the storm raging around them. We don't always have power over our circumstances, but we *do* have the power to choose our response. An attitude of gratitude changes our perspective, leads us to worship, and finds a peace that passes understanding.

I can easily fall into the trap of thanking God merely for His gifts rather than for who He *is*. My father used to say that sometimes he felt like a bank. We kids only came to him when we wanted money. I think we do this with God. "Thanks for this and that and could you add these things too?" As if God were a cosmic vending machine instead of a person who desires communion and conversation with us. Lately I'm trying to move beyond my litany of things that I'm grateful for (my husband, good health, family, and friends) and make an effort to thank God for His *character* attributes. That He is holy and perfect. That He isn't just

loving but He *is* love itself (1 John 4:8, 16). That His mercy is new every morning. That He is in control and His timing is always perfect (even if it's not according to *my* daily planner). Focusing on these concrete things builds my trust in His character and faith for my future. It transforms my worries into worship.

I try to make a point to be grateful to God throughout the day for the small stuff—which isn't so small when you think about going without. I marvel at having eyes to see the sunset, legs to walk the beach, and ears to hear the meadowlark. Then when a sacrifice of praise is called for, I'm able to do it with the right attitude. Because I know even though things aren't currently going the way I'd like them to, I can offer God praise for who He is and not what I want—or don't want—in life. I *can* be grateful. Like the poem below shows (which was written by a woman who was dying of leukemia), it could be otherwise.

> I got out of bed
> On two strong legs.
> It might have been
> otherwise. I ate
> cereal, sweet
> milk, ripe, flawless
> peach. It might
> have been otherwise.
> I took the dog uphill

to the birch wood.
All morning I did
the work I love.
At noon I lay down
with my mate. It might
have been otherwise.
We ate dinner together
at a table with silver
candlesticks. It might
have been otherwise.
I slept in a bed
in a room with paintings
on the walls, and
planned another day
just like this day.
But one day, I know,
it will be otherwise.[3]

~ *Purple Martin* ~

I'll never win the Suzy Homemaker award, because I'm not a good maintenance person. If the white-gloved cleanliness committee comes by my house, most mornings I'll flunk. If it's a sunny day, the dishes in the sink can wait. I'd rather be gardening, walking the beach, or riding my bike. I floss like crazy two weeks before my dental appointments, but in between, I'm sporadic. Neither Tom nor I likes to pay the bills. His argument is that he's a busy executive. My excuse is that I'm a busy person who's not genetically wired for organizational types of activities. I even have personality tests to prove it. I score highest on creativity and lowest on methodical, maintenance-type stuff. Even though I use a timesaving computer program that works well, it still is hard to commit the time and get the bills paid. Consequently, I've picked up our telephone only to discover that the phone company didn't appreciate my lackadaisical approach to paying bills. I'd like to flick a well-manicured hand and say, like Leona Helmsley, "Paying taxes is for the little people." But unfortunately, the IRS views me as the "little people." Maintenance, in some areas, is nonnegotiable.

Birds don't care if your personality type is popular, powerful, perfectionist, or peacemaker; they have non-negotiable needs too. These needs are food, shelter, and water. When it comes to purple martins, they need a maintenance-minded landlord.

This isn't an onerous job, because it's more like a hobby. Or you can think of it as giving a summer-long party to some entertaining friends from South America. You can be an active landlord, providing nesting material and food and keeping an eye out for intruders, or you can be passive, putting the box up when the martins return in the spring and taking it down when they leave in the fall. Like most adventures in life, you get out of it what you put into it.

Purple martins like to nest in colonies. So if you go to the store to buy a purple martin nesting box, you will encounter something that resembles a miniature hotel. You can use this or make your own by putting several hollowed-out gourds together, as Native Americans used to do and more people are doing today. These colonies used to be provided by our natural habitat—old woodpecker holes and rock ledges—but due to encroaching civilization and the diligent efforts of birding enthusiasts, purple martins now prefer human-supplied housing. In fact, they are dependent upon our goodwill.

Because of the introduction of the house sparrow in 1853 and the European starling in 1880 to North America, our native purple martins have to compete for nesting cavities with these birds. While the martins migrate to South America each fall, the sparrows and starlings stick around and so have first pick on the nesting sites each spring. That's where we come in.

Diligent maintenance of your purple martin colony will ensure that sparrows and starlings do not take it over year round. One way to prevent competitors from nesting in your purple martin housing is to figure out when the martins are due to arrive in your backyard and put out the nesting box then. A great map for checking out predicted dates for spring arrival is *www.purplemartin.org* and click on "scout/subadult arrival study." *Www.birdwatchers.com* is another good site for learning about purple martins and buying housing and equipment. If you want to be a more involved landlord, periodically check out each nesting spot to make sure there are no sparrows or starlings and remove their nests if they have infiltrated the site.[1] Gourds are a great housing choice

[1]Bird Watcher's Digest Press has a book called *Enjoying Purple Martins More—the Martin Landlord's Handbook*, 800-879-2473.

because neither sparrows nor starlings like their swaying motion. This doesn't bother the purple martins at all.

Martins like to nest in broad open areas. Meadows, rivers, swamps, lakes, and pastures are all preferred areas. You don't have to be out in the country; residential areas work well if the housing is placed in an open area, particularly near water. I grew up in the suburbs near a lake, and nearly everyone who lived on the lake had an active and entertaining purple martin house in their backyard. Find the biggest open area and put the martin house in the middle of it. Ideally the area should be forty to fifty feet square and within one hundred feet of your house. They like to be near people.

Initially it was believed that purple martins were mosquito-eating machines. Most people in our neighborhood had purple martin houses because of their mythic mosquito-eating reputation. In the Midwest, this is no small thing. I remember T-shirts in both Minnesota and Wisconsin promoting the mosquito as the state bird. The mosquitoes are numerous, they are large, and they are out for blood. Providing housing for a bird that would eat them all and perform entertaining aerial acrobatics was too good a deal to pass up.

Unfortunately, the purple martins are not the mosquito-gobblers that we thought they were. Studies have shown they prefer larger insects such as moths, beetles, wasps, dragonflies, mayflies, and butterflies. Plus, purple martins hunt for their food most often at heights around one hundred feet in the air, which is not where the mosquitoes hang out (on your legs or in your bedroom late at night). But still, I like that the martins eat wasps and moths and perform delightful aerial displays. Also, they can drink *and* bathe while in flight. While flying low over open water, a martin can plunge its breast several times into the water and then fly to a perch to preen and dry off.

Another unique and interesting feat they perform is the dawn song. After the adult males have mated with females and nesting has begun, they start to advertise to other martins that their colony is a fabulous place to live. They do this by performing the dawn song. Each morning before daybreak, adult males fly above the colony site and sing loudly to attract other martins to the colony. This dawn song can be heard for up to thirty square miles and is very successful at attracting other martins. If you don't have any martins using your new colony, you can buy a recording of this dawn song and play it to attract them to your neck of the woods.

Whenever I meet people whose faith just sings out in joy no matter how tough their circumstances, I know that they have attended to the maintenance of their spiritual life. This isn't something we can buy or imitate like the dawn song. This is the fruit of mindful maintenance. If we want more out of our faith than falling asleep in the pew, if we want joy, daily peace of mind, power in prayer, and influence in others' lives, we need to be good landlords to that which has been entrusted to us.

Too often, I think, believers—particularly evangelicals—get caught in a Club Jesus mentality. It's as if we've joined a social club. We think that if we give mental assent to the historical facts, partake in rituals, utter the right words or oath, are sincere in our hearts, *ta da!* Everything is hunky-dory forever after, no maintenance needed. Technically, if we do make a decision with our heart and our head and pray acknowledging that we are a sinner and need the saving grace of Jesus Christ, we are "fireproofed." But that doesn't mean we'll have a life of vibrancy, power, peace, or influence. Those benefits come with sweat and effort and are the result of being tested and found mature.

It's funny, I didn't have any problem realizing that if I wanted to win swim races in my youth, I'd have to put in a lot of long, tedious, difficult workouts. But somehow in my spiritual life I don't apply the same principles. I want God to be the Great Magician, not the Great Physician.

For swimming I ran the extra mile (I *hated* running), lifted weights, and ran stadium stairs until I felt nauseous with exhaustion. In the summer I worked out in the same pool lane as the university men's team—at times terrifying and grueling. Sometimes I worked out three times a day. I knew the price of success; it was concentrated effort. And it paid off. I got a swimming scholarship and did well. But my success wouldn't have happened if I thought I could just join the team, utter an oath to its principles, and then sit back and hope the coach could work his magic on me.

We see the principle in marriage as well. There's more to marriage than saying our beliefs and dreams on the wedding day. We then have to work them out, purposely, within our daily lives for love to blossom and grow.

Even the apostle Paul had work to do. He had been a murderer of Christians, seeking them out and having them put to death. But after the occasion of his dramatic conversion on the road to Damascus had faded into the past, he didn't just sit back and reminisce on that wonderful moment. He had to get down to the hard work and everyday-ness of working out his salvation with "fear and trembling." Spouting a prayer from a booklet or attending a revival crusade won't end our struggles, tough circumstances, or most importantly, need for growth and maturity. Peter too found that one declaration of faith in a moment in time ("You are the Christ") didn't absolve him from the sweaty, heart-pounding growth that is required to move from milk to meat. Our witness to the world is severely compromised when we carry the attitude of "Just say this prayer and you're in the club!" and then we go live carelessly. Gossip, gluttony, materialism, pride, envy, and all sorts of sinful behavior oozes out of us, and we blithely respond to the watching world, "I'm not perfect, just forgiven!" We use that as a license because we are not willing to curb our behaviors and appetites. But God calls us to be different. Romans 12:2 says, "Do not conform any longer to the pattern of this world, but be transformed by the renewing of your mind. Then you will be able to test and approve what God's will is—his good, pleasing and perfect will."

You can tell those who aren't winging it and are truly transformed when it comes to their faith. They demonstrate love, faith, and maturity in action. Mother Teresa, in the streets of Calcutta, never had a Four Spiritual Laws pamphlet or went to a crusade meeting. Persecuted Christians in China suffering for their faith don't have the *Prayer of Jabez,* yet they are seeing their territory expanding—thousands are coming to Christ. Corrie ten Boom in the Nazi concentration camps sang praise songs to Jesus for a crust of bread. I would be whining, "You're the Almighty God. Get me OUTTA here!" These people shame my paper-thin faith. Too often when God decides to mature me by sending tough times, I want to stick my thumb in my mouth and crumple in the corner. Even though I know that we don't get spiritual muscles until we have to carry a burden, and we don't build character until we deal with tough times, I still want to be lazy and take the easy way out. But then I find myself overwhelmed by life's circumstances and wishing I had done a better job in recent months of renewing my mind.

So how can we be better landlords of this faith that's been entrusted to us? We can do the same thing we do for purple martins. Provide ourselves a good home. Find a place where people come together in harmony to learn more about Jesus. If we find a church where we're not growing, we need to find another one. Eat spiritual food. Feasting on garbage TV shows and magazines is going to leave us perpetually dissatisfied and hungry. Learn God's Word. Take a Bible study course. "So then faith comes by hearing, and hearing by the word of God" (Romans 10:17 NKJV). And finally, water our faith with service. The common denominator between Mother Teresa, the persecuted church in China, and Corrie ten Boom is service. Our faith is watered and we flourish when we reach out to others in love. We think good times and comfort will make us happy. But history shows that the people who are filled with the most joy and contentment are those who reach out to others—despite tough times.

When we treat our spiritual life maintenance as non-negotiable the way we do the care and feeding of our physical life, we will have peace of mind, power in prayer, and influence in others' lives. Then no matter what our personality type or the circumstances we find ourselves in, we will be able to rise up and sing our own dawn song.

～ Cardinal ～

My husband had a secret weapon when he courted me. When I discovered this, all my silly arguments about how he probably wasn't the right man for me were torn asunder and my knees went weak. I no longer minded that he was two inches shorter than I was. I ceased to care that he was thirteen years older than I was. And I feigned ignorance that he, in fact, weighed a few pounds less than I did.

His secret weapon wasn't the romantic cards and flowers (although I appreciated them). It wasn't our heartfelt and tender discussions (although they made me cry with happiness). It wasn't his poetry or even the five-hour phone calls (I like creativity and stamina in a man). It was the fact that he could cook like a Cordon Bleu chef *without a recipe*.

Although my mother is incredibly creative and talented

in many areas (as well as being a great artist), she didn't get much in the way of cooking lessons. Whenever she tried to help in the kitchen, my grandmother shooed her out of her way. I grew up thinking that cookies from scratch meant we thawed the tube of dough we bought at the supermarket and sliced it. The idea of starting with flour, sugar, and eggs was as remote as grinding corn with a mortar and pestle. Dinners were shaked and baked, thawed in boiling water, or warmed from a can. And thanks to my parents' busy social schedule, I've probably had every form of TV dinner that Swanson ever produced.

When Tom would casually open up his refrigerator and mutter, "Hmmm, what have we here?" I assumed he was examining various stages of mold and decay that the stereotypical bachelor has in his refrigerator. But no, he was seeing what odds and ends he had in the meat and vegetable drawers that he could whip together into a mouth-watering delight. I would perch on a kitchen stool and stare with amazement as my magician created succulent sauces, perfect pastas, tongue-caressing custards, and decadent desserts. I knew he was smart—but now I knew he was *gifted*. And I also knew he had won my heart.

The male cardinal also uses this secret to courting and winning the heart of his mate. You can often view this behavior, called mate-feeding, at your own birdfeeder. He starts by selecting the plumpest of berries or the most savory seed, then hops over and gallantly tilts his head sideways to

place it in the female cardinal's beak. According to Donald and Lillian Stokes's book *Guide to Bird Behavior*, this can take place as often as four times a minute.

I've always had a soft spot in my heart for the cardinal. When the landscape is frozen and buried under snow and winter seems like it will continue forever, the brilliant red of the male cardinal always gladdens my heart. His distinctive call, *se-vere, se-vere, se-vere,* is easily recognized and one of the first ones my mother taught me. I'm not the only one who is a huge fan of this handsome bird. Nearly every bag of birdseed you buy, many of the bird motifs on Christmas plates and holiday cards, and even my outdoor thermometer display the image of the popular red cardinal. Now that I live in California, where there are no cardinals, I have a realistic cardinal ornament I place in our Christmas tree every year. The cardinal was the first bird to be given official state recognition when Kentucky designated it as their state bird in

1926. Subsequently, seven other states have claimed it as their state bird as well.

With his rich crimson color, jaunty crest on top of his head, and striking black face for contrast, you'd think all he'd need to do is strut his handsome self in front of his intended to win her favor. Not so.

In the winter, the male cardinal is pretty much indifferent, if not hostile, to the female cardinal. Usually a loner, he will chase her off of a feeder and not at all be conciliatory toward her. In the spring, however, a young cardinal's fancy turns to thoughts of love.

Not only does he participate in mate-feeding, where he gallantly feeds her, but the male cardinal also partakes in counter-singing with her. Unlike most birds, where only the male has the distinctive song, the male and female cardinals can sing equally well. In counter-singing, the cardinals perch in different areas and sing to each other. One sings a phrase and then the other cardinal sings it back to his or her mate, matching the phrase. After a while, one switches the tune a little bit and the mate still matches this when she sings it back. This is my idea of a good time. Somebody to feed me delectable delights and sing sweet songs of love to me. Or just mirror back to me that all my utterances are brilliant. I am, I admit, a compliment junkie.

If I happen to walk downstairs all dressed up for a party and Tom fails to immediately praise me on my effort, I'll fill in the blanks for him. Stopping at the foot of the stairs for impact, I'll turn slightly and say in a dramatic voice, "Ohhhh, Laurie! You look just faaaabulous in that outfit! And you wore my favorite color too! How thoughtful of you." Tom's head will snap around and he'll pick up the cue. "Ohhh, Laurie!" he'll say, mimicking my thespian delivery with a grin. "You *do* look wonderful and I *do* appreciate that you wore my favorite color!" And when Tom's feeling the need to hear appreciative comments, he'll "sing" to me, "Oh, Tom, you've emptied the dishwasher *and* cleaned up the kitchen! How wonderful you are!" We usually end up laughing with each other over our Grand Canyon of need to be appreciated and romanced.

We all like to be appreciated, admired, and talked to in an uplifting way. And we all understand the Golden Rule—do unto others as you would have them do unto you. Why, then, is it so hard to do? Why don't we feed each other morsels of hope and encouragement? Why don't we sing songs of love and approval to each other? Why are we so quick to criticize and cut down instead of encourage and inspire?

I know I've married a wonderful, brilliant, and talented person, but what comes out of my mouth too often is, "Why can't you ever take out the trash without me having to *ask* you?"

One of my biggest struggles is criticism. I can't seem to go twenty-four hours without correcting Tom in some small way, pointing out how he could have done something ·more to my taste. This, to me, is shocking. It's shocking because I spent many years praying specifically for a wonderful man just like him. I listed for God the character attributes that I wanted. God delivered on every single one. He even added some I didn't ask for: unending patience, self-control, and heart-melting kindness. Why, then, would I tear it all down with criticism? Why would I act like the foolish woman in Proverbs 14 who tears down her house with her own hands (v.1)?

I'm not the only one. My friend tells me that frequently in her neighborhood the women will get together over lunch and complain about their husbands. I also see criticism or henpecking prevalent among older ladies. I have observed them "tsk-tsking" their husbands for leaving out books and newspapers when company has arrived (in front of the company). They criticize their husbands' actions, too-frequent golfing schedules, and just about anything else you can think of—usually in front of their guests. This makes me cringe. Not because I think they are worse than I am, but because I can clearly see how awfully sharp I would be at criticizing and demeaning my husband by the time I reached their ages. If I continued in the path I was on, I would earn a black belt in tongue-lashing.

I think it's interesting that this is such a common pitfall for women. Indeed, it fits right in for the enemy of our soul's plans to ruin marriage. One of men's greatest needs is to be respected. When we nag and complain that he didn't load the dishwasher correctly (my personal favorite), sort the laundry the right way, or get exactly the birthday gift we wanted, we are paving the way for our own loss of intimacy and romance. At the workplace and with their friends men get approval and rewards; at home they get recrimination and correction. If I were a man, I know which one I'd be tempted to choose.

However, this bent toward criticizing is not limited to women. I've seen retired men who have nothing better to do than follow their wives around the house, commenting on how they could do everything differently or better. This is despite the fact that she has been handling things smoothly for many years before he got on the scene and decided to impart his wisdom. I have another friend who is scrupulously neat and tidy (despite young children underfoot), but if she so much as leaves one item on the counter, her husband is quick to point it out. Criticism, it seems, is an equal-opportunity destroyer.

Solomon knew what he was talking about when he said, "The tongue that brings healing is a tree of life, but a deceitful tongue crushes the spirit" (Proverbs 15:4). I like the way the Living Bible states it: "Gentle words cause life and health; griping brings discouragement." How quickly I can crush romance, affection, tenderness, and all the good things I want in our marriage with my sharp tongue. James too remarked upon the power of the tongue. He said,

> Or take ships as an example. Although they are so large and are driven by strong winds, they are steered by a very

small rudder. . . . Likewise the tongue is a small part of the body, but it makes great boasts. Consider what a great forest is set on fire by a small spark. The tongue also is a fire, a world of evil among the parts of the body. It corrupts the whole person, sets the whole course of his life on fire, and is itself set on fire by hell. . . . No man can tame the tongue. It is a restless evil, full of deadly poison. With the tongue we praise our Lord and Father, and with it we curse men, who have been made in God's likeness. (James 3:4–6, 8–9)

Clearly, we've had a problem with the tongue since day one. What can we do to get back to feeding hope and encouragement to our mates and our loved ones and friends?

Tom nailed the answer to this one day when after a few rounds of criticism from me he asked, "What have you been thinking about today?" I knew what he meant.

My thoughts must have been filled with negative things for all this venom to be spilling out onto him. I mentally reviewed the tracks of my thought life. Morning: *Great, Tom, thanks for leaving your dishes in the sink — too much trouble to put them in the dishwasher? I'm busy and I've got deadlines too, you know! Oh, you're at work and you forgot your wallet? You are so scatterbrained sometimes. Grrr, you didn't take out the garbage like I've asked you a thousand times. If you* cared *about me you'd remember and do it. . . .* Evening: *Go ahead, just leave your coat on the chair instead of hanging it up. I know I'll be putting it away in the morning. Why do you always do that? Dinner's ready and you're on the phone on a business call, you are always in the middle of something important. You expect me to cook and clean up after din-ner? I'm tired too. Do you think I sit around and eat bonbons all day?*

When I fill my head with these negative thoughts, when I savor them and ruminate on them, my tongue is bound to unleash darts and barbs. I could put a muzzle on my mouth, but that doesn't stop the dark thoughts from ricocheting around my brain, coloring my outlook on life. The fact is, Tom cooks most of the meals and cleans up after me a lot. To counteract my brooding and distorted thoughts, I employ two tactics.

First of all, I pay attention to my thought life. When I listen to myself slide down into character assassination mus-ings, I purposely start listing the things about that person I admire and am thankful for. I purposely think about all the good things and habits that person has. For instance, Tom is not a handyman, so when things break I am usually in charge of fixing them (either by sweat or by check). But instead of carping on the fact that I think he's missing an essential fix-it gene, I note to myself how wonderful it is that he writes me poetry, or I think about his sense of humor. Second, when correction or advice is needed, just as I used to do when I coached a swim team or worked in an office, I try to "sandwich" the negative between two positive com-ments. This makes it easier to hear and digest—and I make sure the positive is meatier than the negative.

The importance of training our thought life to master our tongues and achieve harmony isn't a new idea. Philippians 4:8–9 states, "Whatever is true, whatever is noble, whatever is right, whatever is pure, whatever is lovely, whatever is admirable—if anything is excellent or praiseworthy— think about such things. Whatever you have learned or received or heard from me, or seen in me—put it into practice. And the God of peace will be with you."

Are your relationships a little dark and chilly? Want more peace? Use the secret weapons of the cardinal—like sweet counter-singing—and you'll be surprised how fast things warm up.

~ *Roosting* ~

Her voice sounded tremulous and on the edge of tears. "I've just left him and I need a place to stay for a weekend or—or a while." A weekend or a while? *How long is a while?* I wondered. But fortunately, my long-standing friendship with Suzanne caused my mouth to operate before I thought about it and said, "Of course you can stay with us. Whatever we can do to help."

It's scary when a friend is going through hard times. You want to give advice, tell her what's worked for you, but you're afraid of sermonizing and causing her to turn away. Through trial and much error, I've discovered the most effective approach is to be available with a listening ear. To be there for friends without comment, whether what they are doing is crazy or sane, is the first step toward healing and

growth. I've found that if I keep my mouth shut and listen for a few days, then they are more likely to listen later. This does not come to me naturally; I'm an opinionated yakker. Always eager to give my opinion, asked for or not. But thankfully, I'm married to a man who taught me the better way.

Several hours later, we peered out the front window as she parked her car. "Wow!" said Tom. "What all does she *have* in that car? It's stuffed to the roof. *How long* did you say she was staying?"

I turned to him, " 'A weekend or *a while,*' she said."

My friend Suzanne's definition of *a while* ended up being a month or two. The difference between when she arrived and when she finally went back to her husband was remarkable.

She burst through the front door that first day declaring, "Don't you *dare* tell me to go back to him. I want a divorce. Don't try to change my mind or I'll leave. I don't want anything to do with him! I hate him. And don't talk to me about God either. If God is who my husband says He is, well then, I *hate* God!" Obviously we were concerned. Wisely, my husband squeezed my arm as a reminder to be quiet, and we just listened. Several nights later over dinner, as the litany of her husband's shortcomings was being reviewed for what seemed like the hundredth time, we cut her short.

"Suzanne," I said, "we don't really care as much about your marriage status so much as we care about your *relationship to God.* Let's stop talking about *Gary* and talk about who

God is. We want you to fall back in love with God. That's our main concern. Once that's sorted out, everything else will take care of itself."

We wanted her to know she was loved no matter what she chose and that we were there for her. Of course we were very concerned. But after she realized we weren't going to kick her out unless she professed that she would stay married, she calmed down and began to listen. And in time, her faith in God was restored, she was strengthened, and she returned to Gary.

This wasn't the first time Tom had provided a safe haven for someone in need. Years ago in his twenties he had come across a homeless man named Steve who was living out of an abandoned ambulance. Tom invited him to dinner and eventually invited him to move in with him. After some months passed, Steve decided he wanted to be a follower of Jesus. Then Steve went on to finish high school and get his GED. He married his long-term girlfriend and went on to seminary. Pretty amazing for a guy who used to be aimless and homeless. Makes me wonder how many people we run across each day who need a little haven where they can renew their strength. If I'm honest with myself, I have to admit that I tend to pass them by and think, *They really need to shape up and get a job*.

The Bible has strong words about this kind of attitude. "If anyone has material possessions and sees his brother in need but has no pity on him, how can the love of God be in him?" (1 John 3:17). I used to rationalize, "Whatever money I give this homeless person, he'll just spend it on drugs and alcohol, so forget it. I'm not wasting my money." Then I started offering to buy them food instead. But after a while I realized what I really was doing was trying to control their lives, making sure they didn't buy drugs or anything I didn't approve of. I was giving them what I thought they needed (just as I do with friends at times). But now I follow my stepdaughter Michelle's advice. She said, "It's not my responsibility or problem what they do with the money that I give them. They're responsible before God for that. My job is to be loving, faithful, and give what I can."

I'm so glad Jesus didn't demand the woman at the well shape up before he helped her. It was a hot, dusty day and she was alone at the well drawing water. It's interesting to note that she was alone because normally women in the Middle East would go to the well in groups or go together to the river to wash their clothes. But this woman was probably alone because of her lifestyle. She had had five husbands and the man she was currently living with was not her husband. She wasn't the sort of woman whom the other women in the neighborhood wanted to associate with. She was also a Samaritan, a group of people that ancient Jews would have nothing to do with, much less speak to. But Jesus, despite being Jewish, spoke to her. He treated her with love and compassion.

Instead of saying, "Hey, you hussy, I know what you've

been up to, sleeping around with all those men!" He first met her emotional and spiritual needs. *Then* she was open to listening to Him. Then she was desirous of changing her life. Jesus provided a safe place for her to be herself and converse with Him. Can you imagine her response if He had said, "Why don't you reform your lifestyle, join a women's Bible study, help out at the local soup kitchen, and dress a little more conservatively? Then I think you'll be ready to receive my nuggets of wisdom and help." She probably would have told him to buzz off! And in fact, that's what most of the world is telling holier-than-thou Christians who try to get everyone to behave according to their expectations. Once people know that with us they are safe and free from judgment and that we want to serve them, they will open up. People don't care how much we *know* until they know how much we *care*.

All of us at some time or another need a safe place where we can get away from the storms of life, huddle with others, and renew our strength. Birds too go through stressful times and need a place of emergency care and shelter. When blizzards, freezing temperatures, hurricanes, or other tough circumstances arise, birds need a place where they can group together in safety. That's where we come in, with roosting boxes.

Roosting boxes are like nesting boxes (or birdhouses), only bigger. That's because a roosting box's sole purpose is to provide shelter and warmth to a group of birds. When bad weather strikes, birds huddle together, combining their body heat to stay warm. Some bluebird fans have seen up to twelve bluebirds smooshed together in a single roosting box. I've also heard about a man in the state of Washington who observed thirty-one winter wrens crowd into his roosting box.

The boxes come in various shapes and sizes. My friend Peter has several three-sided platforms tucked up under the eaves of his house, away from the prevailing winds. He lives in an area that during winter storms has clocked ninety-nine-mile-an-hour winds. His roosting boxes aren't meant for long-term stays, usually just overnight until the worst has passed.

Simply put, a roosting box is bigger than a nesting box and has no ventilation holes. John K. Terres, in his excellent book *Songbirds in Your Garden,* suggests a general size for small birds is ten inches square and about three feet high from floor to roof. The entrance hole is near the bottom of the box so that it prevents heat from escaping. It's a good idea to keep the entrance hole no more than two inches above the floor of the box. Inside there should be several round perches about a quarter-inch in diameter and staggered, so that a dozen or so birds can roost together and share body heat. Mount your roosting box eight to ten feet off the ground and away from the prevailing winds. It's also a good idea to include a predator baffle to protect the birds from squirrels and raccoons. On very cold nights, birds' metabolisms slow down and they become extremely vulnerable in this state.

At some time or another we find ourselves in a vulnerable state. Life has battered us around and we just need a safe haven to get our strength back. Sometimes it's as simple as lunch with a friend who won't sermonize. Sometimes it may mean a place where we can huddle in the warmth of friends. Sometimes it may mean rolling out the couch for a friend for a while. We can be men and women after God's own heart when we show compassion for others and provide roosting boxes for the storms of life.

Who knows? We may need one ourselves one day.

～ Cowbird ～

For a long time Tom and I have considered adopting a child. And for a long time, I was worried that I wouldn't bond as quickly with an adopted child as I would with a biological child. My sister tried to point out the fallacy of this thinking. She told me, "Right after my first son was born I wasn't filled with ooey-gooey emotions about how wonderful I thought he was. Or how blessed the whole event was. After thirty-six hours of back-breaking labor I looked at him and thought, *So* you're *the little stinker who gave me all that pain!*" Of course, now she's proud of and wildly in love with her oldest son, but her first thoughts upon greeting him in this world weren't sticky bonding thoughts.

Other mothers have told me the same thing. "I was exhausted and frazzled after taking care of a colicky baby," my friend Susan told me. "I wasn't exactly wild about this little screaming machine. I think I really bonded with her one day while changing her diaper. She was a few months old, the colic was dying down, and she smiled at me. The sun finally broke through." This gives me hope. This means I don't have the pressure to give birth or bond within the first moments in order to love and care for a child.

My other worry was that if the child had any serious emotional problems (or rejected me), I would have thoughts like, *This is too hard. I think I got the wrong baby. I want to give him back, thank you very much.* All my friends who have children laugh at me about this. "Trust me," they say. "We *all* want to give back our kids at difficult times. Just because you gave birth doesn't change the fact that sometimes they can be challenging." Okay, I see now that most of my worries are normal struggles in parenting, so the only hurdle I have left is whether or not to pursue this adoption route.

It fascinates me to realize that thousands of songbirds around North America have to make this same decision every spring. Robins, cardinals, sparrows, blue jays, and many other songbirds also have an adoption decision to make. That's because these birds discover that a foreign egg has been laid in their nest. A cowbird egg, to be specific.

The female cowbird is the bad girl of the bird world. In appearance she is small, brown, quiet, and not very brazen. But in behavior she's wearing too-tight clothing, fishnet stockings, and heavy black eyeliner and is smoking long cigarettes. Like Ado Annie in *Oklahoma,* she's the bird whose song is, "I'm jest a girl who can't say no!"

Unlike other birds who match up with a partner each spring, the female cowbird has many partners. In the Midwest farmlands, male cowbirds are not territorial, so they hang together in small flocks in a fixed area. Meanwhile, the females are out roaming for handsome males and shopping for host nests in which to lay their eggs. And busy birds they are. The female cowbird will lay an average of about forty eggs per breeding season, and rarely more than one egg per nest. In the deciduous forests of the East Coast, the females are not quite so promiscuous. Here the females have fixed territories and the males do more of the roaming. But the male must still be on guard and stay near his female, because if he doesn't, she will mate with whatever male is close by.

The males aren't flashy; most have brown heads and black bodies with a slight green tint. There are also shiny cowbirds and bronzed cowbirds that don't have the brown head, but in either case, they aren't much to look at. Maybe that's why the male cowbirds need to go to great lengths to "display" for these eager females, and their courtship antics are interesting to watch. The moves in the males' repertoire include what the Stokes's guide[1] calls bill-tilt, song, and topple-over. This last display consists of the male bird fluffing out his

[1]Donald and Lillian Stokes, *Guide to Bird Behavior,* Volume Two (New York: Little, Brown and Company, 1983), 213.

body feathers, arching his neck, spreading his tail and wings, and then falling forward—sort of an elaborate, deep bowing action. (I know a lot of women who would appreciate that behavior in a suitor or husband.) Giving song is what it sounds like, singing. And bill-tilt is when the bird lifts his head and points his bill up to the sky. Bill-tilt makes him look like he's gazing at the heavens for directions, but he's fooling the female; he would never ask for directions. He's only displaying.

After the female mates with a male who displays such behavior, she needs to go nest shopping. Just like women around the world, she prefers to do this alone and without him hanging over her shoulder, assessing her every move. Whenever Tom wants to hurry me along when I'm shopping, he stays close behind me—right on my heels. This doesn't create a conducive environment for leisurely browsing through antique stores, so I try to get him engaged else-where. "Hey!" I say with mock enthusiasm, "isn't that a used bookstore across the street?" Tom feels about bookstores the way most women do about a sale at the shoe store. He'll be gone for hours. I don't know what the female cowbird tells the male to dissuade him, but if he does try to follow her she becomes aggressive and chases him off.

The female is very sly in how she goes about finding a host nest. Some mornings you can find her quietly sitting in the treetops, keenly observing what's going on around her, looking for potential nests. Another tactic she employs is to softly move among the shrubbery or walk on the forest floor to view where birds are energetically building nests. Her third approach is to fly into the shrubbery making a lot of noise and flapping her wings. This is probably designed to frighten out the nesting birds and make their locations more obvious. She's got to continue using her sharp observation tactics throughout the breeding season in order to find nests to lay her eggs in. After she lays her egg in the nest, she's done. Now the host bird who built the nest must raise the young cowbird.

Sometimes the host bird discovers the offending egg when she comes back to the nest. In this case, the host bird punctures the foreign egg and gets rid of it. Or she will desert the nest or build another one on top of the existing nest. Some birds, however, don't seem to mind or notice that there is a foreign egg in their nest. These birds willingly accept and adopt the cowbird egg and incubate it along with their own eggs.

It seems unfair to me that God would allow the female cowbird to break all the rules while other birds are so diligent, going to great lengths to build a solid nest and responsibly raise a brood. She doesn't mate with one bird; she mates with as many as she can. She doesn't build a nest; she pirates the use of other, industrious workers' nests. She doesn't care for her baby birds; she lets the host birds do all the work. In the bird world, this is unique and appalling behavior. No other songbird acts this way. And yet, God seems to love this bird, to have a purpose for her, because He created her and allows her to continue pursuing her wanton, irresponsible lifestyle.

Like the prodigal son's older brother, I am annoyed when people who behave poorly get life's blessings. When we were desperate to get pregnant, the newspapers were full of stories about drug-addicted mothers having babies or high-school kids throwing away their newborns in Dumpsters. This drove me crazy. I wanted to repeatedly bang my head against the wall in frustration. I couldn't understand why God could allow this sort of unfairness. This wasn't the kind of God I wanted running things or my life.

Then Tom pointed out to me all the people he's helped in their careers. Many of them have gone on to glorious fame and exceeding fortune, even though they may not be brilliant or have not earned a Ph.D., as Tom has. They are not self-sacrificing or as hardworking, and some of them don't even believe in God. It certainly didn't seem fair. Knowing I wasn't alone made me feel a little bit better. But then Tom had to go and give me truth, which made me feel uncomfortable.

"The only reason you're angry," he said, "is because you feel you *deserve* something. You think you'd be a better mother. You think you deserve a child more than they do."

"Yeah, and your point is?"

"Well, imagine you're told you have a terminal illness and
you have only three months to live. You can spend those last
months in Paris. Then they suddenly found a cure and said,
'Congratulations! You'll live! But you don't get the trip to
Paris.' Would you even care about that trip? No. When it
comes right down to it, we deserve death. But because of
Jesus taking on our sins at the cross, we get life. Anything
beyond that is just icing on the cake. You'll have more joy in
life if you focus on the blessings you *do* have instead of what
you *don't* have."

I hate it when he's right.

But this wasn't news to me. I should've known better.
God told Moses, "I will have mercy on whom I will have
mercy, and I will have compassion on whom I will have compassion" (Exodus 33:19). And again in the New Testament
we are told, "He causes his sun to rise on the evil and the
good, and sends rain on the righteous and the unrighteous"
(Matthew 5:45). If I'm honest with myself, I have to admit I
want mercy for *me* and justice for everyone else.

In the midst of my shaking my fist at God, I came across
Romans 9:20: "But who are you, O man, to talk back to
God? 'Shall what is formed say to him who formed it, "Why
did you make me like this?" ' " It gave me a picture of my
puny self, with my back to the cliff's edge, squawking,
demanding, and complaining but forgetting that I had nowhere else to go. I wasn't in a bargaining position. And if

that wasn't enough, Psalm 73 was. Particularly verses 21 and 22: "When my heart was grieved and my spirit embittered, I was senseless and ignorant; I was a brute beast before you." I think I'm using all my college-educated faculties and logic when I complain and question God's working in my life. He thinks otherwise.

This year, as songbirds across this continent are adopting and taking care of eggs that are not theirs, maybe I could choose to stop complaining about the circumstances that have landed in my nest and adopt God's plan for my life. When I assimilate the message of my feathered friends, then I'll experience God's wings of mercy, when *His* good plans for my life take flight.

~ Chickadee ~

Below-zero temperatures made for magical mornings where I grew up. I would wake up to intricate, prehistoric-looking patterns on my frosted bedroom windows. Overnight, the freezing weather had created wondrous crystalline ferns and scrolls over the glass. They crawled and meandered across the windowpanes, each window with its own eerie design. The pale, weak winter sun barely penetrated the exotic icy artwork.

Padding downstairs to breakfast, I could smell the lingering woodsmoke from last night's fire. In the kitchen, my mother would have hot cereal sprinkled with brown sugar waiting to fortify me for the trek to the school-bus stop. While eating my breakfast I would look out the kitchen window and see our backyard, so different from the lush, humid green of summer, now a landscape of barren trees with ice-coated fingers clawing into the dim gray skies. Everything was blanketed with snow. The picnic table was buried. The birdbath was entombed. The lilac bushes were bent over, buckling under the weight of the snow. There was a loud silence to the cold. Nothing moved; the icy air seemed to sap the energy from every living thing. Even the dog wouldn't go outside, it was so frigid. He'd whine to go out and then after stepping onto the porch, tuck his tail and whine to *not* go out. It was *twenty below zero,* after all.

Once breakfast was over, my mother would faithfully trudge through the snow to our birdfeeder. She'd fill up the feeder and then sprinkle some birdseed on the ground near her statue of St. Francis of Assisi. The first bird to the feeder would inevitably be the brave little black-capped chickadee. In fact, my mother swears that sometimes it seemed as if the chickadee was sitting nearby scolding her, "Hurry up! I've been out here waiting all morning for you!"

I think the chickadee is, in a word, *adorable*. Whether they are the black-capped, chestnut-backed, or mountain chickadees, they all have cute little black caps—almost like berets—on top of their heads. They are about the size of a goldfinch (five inches) and weigh only one third of an ounce—or as one person noted, "About as much as a handful of paper clips." Their call is easily identifiable. They seem to be saying their name: *chickadee-dee-dee-dee*. Or a shorter version, *feee-bee, feee-beee*. But what endears the chickadee to me and many others is that the chickadee has got the biggest heart of all the songbirds, despite its tiny size.

Ralph Waldo Emerson called the chickadee a "scrap of valor" for its fearlessness and ability to endure frigid winters. The chickadee is able to fluff up his feathers to make an inch-thick furry coat that provides warmth. Standing outside in twenty-below weather, the difference in temperature between his body and the outside air is 128 degrees. But unlike redpolls and other small birds that can endure cold winters, the chickadee does not have a *crop*, an internal food storage bag. Instead, the chickadee must eat constantly to keep up his fat reserves and strength. On short winter days when there aren't many hours of sunlight, he's got a lot of work to do.

Our "scrap of valor" needs to consume enough calories every day to add 10 percent to his body weight, which he then burns overnight. This is like a 140-pound person eating enough to weigh 154 by day's end (49,000 calories) and then expending that energy overnight for survival so he faces the morning at 140 again. This is where we come in. We can help the chickadee face harsh weather and short days by providing suet and birdseed at our feeders.

The chickadee's ability to survive cold is admirable, but what charms most people is his attitude. The Yiddish equivalent would be *chutzpah*. Tom Brown, who runs a tracker school in New Jersey, says this about the chickadee in his book *The Tracker*: "We learned to be patient observers like the owl. We learned cleverness from the crow, and courage from the jay, who will attack an owl ten times its size to drive it off its territory. But above all of them ranked the chickadee because of its indomitable spirit."[1]

I came across several Web sites where people told stories about the bravery of the chickadee in their backyards. One told how a chickadee tormented and thwarted a squirrel from entering its territory. Another related how a flock of songbirds at his feeders scattered at the sight of a northern shrike (predator bird), but the chickadee led him on a merry chase and outwitted him by flying straight toward a glass storm door and veering off at the last minute. Caught by surprise and unable at that speed to make such a quick turn, the shrike smashed into the door and was unconscious for several minutes. The chickadee perched on a nearby branch and seemed to giggle at his own cleverness and bravery.

What I find most amazing about the chickadee is that of all the songbirds that visit our feeders, he is the one most likely to be taught to feed out of our hand. In many of my

---

[1]Tom Brown, *The Tracker* (New York: Berkley Books, 1979).

birding books I have come across people's experiences with hand-feeding chickadees in their backyards.[2]

Unlike the brave chickadee, I was pretty much a fraidy cat growing up. Despite the fact I was always taller than everyone else and gregarious in nature, I was insecure and shy. When the giant Easter bunny handed out chocolate rabbits at the restaurant where we had brunch, I was too terrified to approach. All the other kids gleefully went forward. I hung back. "Go *on!*" my mother said impatiently. "There's nothing to be afraid of." The Easter bunny was as tall as my mother and had an oversized head. I suspected that there was a person in there, looking out through the bunny's mouth, which was in a permanent grin. Worst of all, the giant bunny was eerily quiet. He never said a word. I wanted a chocolate rabbit, but not enough to brave the mute giant in front of me. My fear had a price. I went home without a chocolate rabbit.

When I lost a tooth, I was terrified of the tooth fairy. "But what if I wake up when he comes," I whined to my older brother, "and he's big and ugly and scary looking?!" I imagined that the tooth fairy might look something like a troll, not Tinker Bell. My brother couldn't believe he was related to anyone as gullible and chicken as I was. "Don't be

---

[2]Information about hand-feeding chickadees can be found in John K. Terres's *Songbirds in Your Garden* (Chapel Hill: Algonquin Books, 1994). Once it is used to your presence, the chickadee can become so bold as to sit on your shoulder or hat for company, whether or not you are feeding him. This reminds me of Henry David Thoreau's comment about a bird alighting on his shoulder: "I felt that I was more distinguished by that circumstance than I should have been by any epaulet I could have worn."

so stupid," he said. "The tooth fairy is just Mom and Dad." Instead of feeling disappointment that a charming childhood myth had been snatched from me, I remember a distinct feeling of relief and gratitude that I didn't have to face the unknown.

At the age of twelve I was afraid to take the bus by myself downtown long after my friends were doing it. I was afraid to kiss boys in high school long after my friends were doing it. And I was afraid to enter into an intimate, personal relationship with the God of the universe, even though I longed to do it.

A cousin sent me a book around my twelfth birthday about Joni Eareckson. Joni was a typical teenager who loved to ride horses and swim. Tragically, she dove into shallow water, broke her neck, and became a quadriplegic. I think my relative meant to encourage me to leave behind the forms of religion I dutifully engaged in on Sunday mornings and grow into a more personal and intimate dialogue with God. I knew this was what I wanted. But Joni had prayed to know God more personally and follow the teachings of Christ, then shortly thereafter, she had her tragic accident. Instead of seeing the book for what it was—a description of how God can work good and positive things even out of tragic circumstances—to me the book said, *Trust this guy and you're toast!*

So I coasted for a few years, longing to know and be

more intimately known by this incredible Creator of heaven and earth and yet terrified to give Him full access to my life. I knew I wanted to move beyond the cold, liturgical religion I was brought up with. I agreed with its historical facts but it didn't influence my daily life. I knew I wanted a relationship where I felt forgiven, accepted, and could pray and see answers to those prayers. But I was afraid. I was afraid that the price was too high.

I feared God would want me to be a missionary in some disease-ridden steamy climate where no one was interested. I feared God would cripple me as Joni had been crippled. Logically, this didn't make any sense, that the One who loves me more than any other heart on this earth or in heaven would purposely seek to do me harm. But at least, I reasoned, He probably wasn't interested in *my* definition of a fun life. So I continued on for a few more years, pursuing my definition of fun. After a while, I decided that *fun* sometimes turned out to mean entrapment, shame, wasting my talents, and going nowhere fast. I wanted to look back over my life and feel that it had meant something, it had been worthwhile, I had achieved something significant. Despite my successful athletic endeavors, I knew that wasn't happening. So one winter day, not long before Christmas, I said, "Okay, I *am* scared of this but I'm going to do it anyway. You can have all of me, Jesus. Come into my heart and take control of my life."

When I look back on that moment of decision now, I

laugh. Not because I wasn't genuine or that a monumental shift in my spiritual life didn't occur, but because I am stunned at what that decision entailed. I guess it was my unspoken belief that God would pretty much pave the way for me after that. A college evangelist once told me, "God has a wonderful plan for your life." I took that to mean I would have quick and definite answers to my prayers, I would see situations improve, and I'd probably see my grades move up a notch. Those things *did* occur sometimes, but they are not the things that caused me to grow in love or wisdom. Trusting Him when life was painful, unfair, and didn't make sense, choosing to obey His Word when it wasn't convenient, and working out my faith with "fear and trembling" (Philippians 2:12) were the messy process that still goes on to this day. It's rarely easy, orderly, or pretty, but the rewards are worth it.

I understand why people are reticent and even fearful to talk to God face-to-face. He's the Big Man upstairs, the guy who holds all the puppet strings. He's the Wizard of Oz, Superman, and all supreme authority figures rolled into one. If we didn't have a particularly close relationship with our father or other authority figures growing up, the idea of getting close to Mr. Big is even more daunting. If God is like our earthly examples, then there is the fear of being hurt, suffering disappointment, or abuse. Trust Him with my hopes, dreams, and heart? Yikes.

Those of us who were raised in organized religion heard,

"Fear God and keep His commandments." Repeatedly we are told to fear God, and we do. We're also aware of our pettiness and multitude of sins, both what we've done and those things we've left undone. He is the perfect and holy Creator of the heavens and the earth. We are prone to wander, full of selfish and sinful desires, and only tend to talk to Him when we're in trouble. It's no wonder we are hesitant to approach Him. But He says He longs for us to do so.

In Isaiah it is recorded, " 'Come now, let us reason together,' says the Lord. 'Though your sins are like scarlet, they shall be white as snow; though they are red as crimson, they shall be like wool' " (1:18). And in Jeremiah God promises He will listen to us. "Then you will call upon me and come and pray to me, and I will listen to you" (29:12). He delights in hearing from us. In fact, God's desire for relationship with us is what the Bible is all about. He's running after us, welcoming us home in the prodigal son story. In the book of Hosea, He's weeping over our leaving Him for other things and people.

I've always loved the illustration of how Christianity is different from all other religions. On a piece of paper, draw two horizontal parallel lines a few inches apart. One represents heaven, where God is. One represents earth, where we are. Draw a stick figure of a person, standing on earth. In all other religions, man is standing on earth, stretching, reaching, longing to draw closer to heavenly things, toward perfection. In Christianity, God stretches down (draw a cross that reaches from heaven to earth) and *reaches out to us*.

Instead of reaching out to Him directly in response, we try other routes. "Pray to your angel" someone told me the other day. TV is full of ads for tarot readings. Others try to use biblical figures and people long dead as go-betweens. I think this is understandable but misguided. Why talk to an intermediary when the president and king has told you to come directly to him? God has told us specifically that we are to turn nowhere else but to Him. "For there is one God and one mediator between God and men, the man Christ Jesus" (1 Timothy 2:5). And in the book of Acts, "Salvation is found in no one else, for there is no other name under heaven given to men by which we must be saved" (Acts 4:12). Nowhere in the Bible do you see God condoning or encouraging us to pray to, petition, or praise anyone else. He also says we should come to Him with boldness and confidence. We're told in the book of Hebrews that we can be bold in drawing near to God: "Let us then approach the throne of grace with confidence, so that we may receive mercy and find grace to help us in our time of need" (Hebrews 4:16).

We can be as brave and bold as the chickadee when we approach God because we have the confidence of His love. He tells us, "I have loved you with an everlasting love; I

have drawn you with loving-kindness" (Jeremiah 31:3). And he promised to receive us: "Whoever comes to me I will never drive away" (John 6:37). Clearly, we can learn from the *chutzpah* of the black-capped chickadee. God wants us to draw near. He will not turn us back, and we can expect good things from His hand.

⌁ Red-Winged Blackbird ⌁

My friends Katie and Mark were out enjoying a walk when Mark noticed a bird.

"What's the name of that red-winged blackbird?" he asked.

"It's a red-winged blackbird," said Katie.

"No, really—what's its *name*?"

"A *red-winged blackbird*! That's its name, Mark."

Many of the birds we find in our backyards are named for what they look like. This is great for the beginning birder because it makes it easy to identify them. The goldfinch is gold. The cardinal is cardinal-red. The bluebird is blue. The black-capped chickadee has a black cap. And the red-winged blackbird looks just like its name. It has red marks on its wings, almost like epaulets, on the top of its black shoulders.

Red-winged blackbirds usually breed around cattail marshes, so you can find them there or in nearby fields. They have a distinctive *kon-ka-reeee* call that they use when they are displaying for a mate. This display consists of spreading their wings and tail while flaring their bright-red epaulets.[1] They look almost like body builders flexing their muscles when they fluff up their red shoulders for the ladies. Spring is the best time to look for this display of the aptly named red-winged blackbird.

Naming things is important. When I was scuba diving, I wanted to know the names of the fish I was seeing. It was exciting to be deep underwater and realize that the clownfish were the ones I found so charming and entertaining. The moorish idols were the shy but elegant ones hiding behind rocks. And the parrotfish were the rainbow-hued ones that made the loud scraping sound as they chewed on the coral. Knowing their names also enabled me to identify the deadly and dangerous ones to stay away from, such as the poisonous lionfish and stonefish. It gave me a feeling of confidence and mastery over my surroundings to know what I was looking at. The same thing happened when I became an obsessed gardener.

It didn't do any good to ask at the local nursery, "Do you have any of those pink spike-like plants?" This could get me all sorts of answers (Gladiola? Liatris? Gaura? Foxglove?

---

[1] David Allen Sibley, *The Sibley Guide to Bird Life and Behavior* (New York: Alfred A. Knopf, 2001).

Snapdragons?) but not the one I wanted: obedient plant. *Physostegia virginiana*. Mark Twain said, "The difference between the right word and the almost-right word is the difference between the lightning and the lightning-bug."

A lot of power and reference is associated with names. For years, Scandinavians named their children "John's son" or "Erick's son," hence Johnson and Erickson. That method of naming told the child's parentage. It indicated what family they belonged to. For Native Americans picking the right name for their children was a solemn and important ceremony. Many tribes waited until the children could walk and their personality became evident. They named their children according to the character and physical traits they possessed. Sometimes our families do this to us informally, and it can take a lifetime to shed the names and labels they give us.

I was always daydreaming as a kid and quite forgetful. I

would be told to go get something for my mother, and then I'd get distracted by a book or some project in my room. She'd come looking for me later wondering what happened to me. Today, people who are easily distracted or whose thoughts are often elsewhere get named Space Cadet and Flake. In my family, I was Out-to-Lunch.

It was a great discovery when I moved to Australia and found that people didn't have preconceived notions of who I was. I learned to think about myself in new ways. My friends Down Under gave me new names and labels such as creative, outgoing, and friendly.

Today I heard someone on the radio admit that she was a fat child and kids used to sing "Piggy Sue" to her. Forty years later she is an accomplished therapist, but the memory is still fresh. Names can carry a great deal of emotional weight and power.

When I worked in advertising, my colleagues would be all bent out of shape if they didn't get a certain title after their name. In ad agencies, titles were many, varied, and handed out like candy. (My motto was always, "Don't praise me—*raise* me!") I see this too in Tom's field of computers and software. Often someone working for him is salivating for a coveted title or position. We associate power and prestige with certain names like *president, vice-president, chief operating officer,* and *senior officer.*

The book of Proverbs says that a good name is more desirable than great riches. And Solomon said that a good name is better than fine perfume. Names are important to God as well. Especially *yours*.

Hagar, the slave, the pawn of Abraham and Sarah's ill-considered plan to bring about a child, flees Sarah's wrath and ends up in the desert. She's alone as she cries in defeat and God comes to her aid. Hagar says to God, "You are the God who sees me" (Genesis 16:13). This is one of my favorite moments in the Bible. No matter how small and insignificant we may feel at times, God sees us. No matter how badly we've blown it or how badly others have treated us, He cares. And He knows us by name. So many times, names are recorded in the Bible of insignificant people whom God doesn't see as insignificant. He calls them by name and gives them dignity and respect. Just a cursory glance through the books of Numbers or Chronicles reveals long lists of names and tribes, each one known to God.

I like the way God gives us names about who we are becoming—our positive possibilities—not based on what we've done. The apostle Paul said that God is "the God who gives life to the dead and calls things that are not as though they were" (Romans 4:17). I like the way God changes the names of people in the Bible too. To the first patriarch He said, "No longer will you be called Abram; your name will be Abraham, for I have made you a father of many nations" (Genesis 17:5).

I also like the account of Jacob wrestling with the man in the book of Genesis. All his life, Jacob (whose name means *deceiver* or *usurper*) had tried to get things done his own way. The night he wrestles with the man, the man asks him his name. I don't think this was for the man's benefit so much as for Jacob's. God seems to be asking, *Who are you really, Jacob?* He knows that Jacob has struggled his whole life with his identity. God wants Jacob to say his name aloud. Then God tells him, "Your name will no longer be Jacob, but Israel, because you have struggled with God and with men and have overcome" (Genesis 32:28). Jacob goes from being named the *usurper* to wearing the name of *overcomer*.

I'm so glad we don't have to wear names based on our behavior. The red-winged blackbird could be called the *polygamous bird,* because he mates with more than one female each season and helps raise several broods. We have names for that in human behavior, names like cad, womanizer, and adulterer.

A brief look at ourselves could reveal some interesting names and titles that we wouldn't want to wear publicly. *She-who-lies-about-how-much-she-spent-shopping* or *She-who-secretly-envies-other-women's-homes* and *He-who-desires-other-men's-wives* are just some of the scary labels we could be named. (I think I'd prefer Running Deer or Babbling Brook.) Thankfully, God doesn't see us this way.

Not only is our name important to God, He wants us to know the importance of *His* name.

The third commandment states, "You shall not misuse the name of the Lord your God, for the Lord will not hold anyone guiltless who misuses his name" (Exodus 20:7). Or another way to put this is, "Do not take the name of the Lord your God in vain." God takes the use of His name seriously. "I am the Lord; that is my name! I will not give my glory to another or my praise to idols" (Isaiah 42:8). The Bible lists many names of God. Here are just a few of them:

El Elyon	The Lord most high	Deut. 26:19
El Shaddai	God all sufficient	Genesis 17:1–2
Jehovah-Roi	The God who sees	Genesis 16:13
Jehovah-Rapha	The Lord our healer	Exodus 15:26
Immanuel	God with us	Isaiah 7:14

These names of God are important because they reveal God's character and heart toward us. Time and time again, the Bible gives examples of people running to safety and accomplishing miracles in the name of the Lord. "The name of the Lord is a strong tower; the righteous run to it and are safe" (Proverbs 18:10). "Our help is in the name of the Lord, the Maker of heaven and earth" (Psalm 124:8). There is *healing* in the name of the Lord; "Is any one of you sick? He should call the elders of the church to pray over him and anoint him with oil in the name of the Lord" (James 5:14). And finally, there is *power and authority* in the name of the Lord Jesus Christ.

When Peter and John encountered the lame man who was begging for money outside the temple Peter said to him,

"Silver or gold I do not have, but what I have I give you. In the name of Jesus Christ of Nazareth, walk" (Acts 3:6). And the man walked away, healed.

One of the most riveting moments I've experienced was when a woman in our church talked about a trip she took to Africa years ago. Her faith was about as strong as you would expect of a young person who hadn't been through any trials or difficult times to test it. While visiting a village one day, she and her group were told that there was a woman who was extremely ill, fading fast. Could their group pray for this sick person? *Well, of course,* they thought (without much faith). They shuffled into her hut, laid hands on her, and prayed. The woman jumped up and exclaimed that she was healed. "We were shocked," Christy admitted. Then, after hearing about the woman who was healed, others in the village came and lined up for prayer. The group, again without much faith, shrugged their shoulders and agreed to pray for them all. Christy said, "To this day I almost don't believe what I saw. We prayed for people in the name of Jesus Christ and they were healed. The blind saw and the lame walked." She readily admits that she and her group didn't have much faith, but they *did* have the name of Jesus. There is power in the name of Jesus.

Paul explains why the name of Jesus has this power:

Who, being in very nature God, did not consider equality with God something to be grasped, but made himself nothing, taking the very nature of a servant, being made in human likeness. And being found in appearance as a man, he humbled himself and became obedient to death — even death on a cross! Therefore God exalted him to the highest place and gave him the name that is above every name, that at the name of Jesus every knee should bow, in heaven and on earth and under the earth, and every tongue confess that Jesus Christ is Lord, to the glory of God the Father. (Philippians 2:6–11)

Names carry great meaning. God never forgets a face or a name, including yours. He says that He has our names inscribed on the palms of his hands (Isaiah 49:16). And in heaven, He will give us a new name as He did Jacob. I'm glad that mine won't be based on how I look, like the red-winged blackbird (She-who-can't-say-no-to-dessert), or based on my behavior (She-who-criticizes-too-much). And because my sins were nailed to the cross with Jesus, I'm confident that one of my new nicknames will be *victorious one*. Yours can be too.

⌐ For the Birds ⌐

When I first attracted birds to my yard, it was by accident. I wasn't interested in birds; I was an obsessed gardener. But as I described in *Gardening Mercies,* my lovely English garden in the backyard was plagued by loud freeway noise. Eight lanes of it, just behind our neighbor's house across the street. Although I loved my garden, listening to all that roaring traffic while I tiptoed through the tulips made me tense. I decided I needed a big water fountain that made a loud, splashing noise to drown out the commuters. I placed it near the house so the sound of the cascading water would be amplified as it echoed off the side of the building. To my surprise I started seeing a significant increase in the number and variety of birds in the garden. They were all attracted to the fountain. Jewel-toned goldfinches and purple finches

flitted about the spray. Hummingbirds hovered and shim-
mied in the sparkling mist, and cedar waxwings stopped by
in droves. I didn't realize that the sound of water could be
such a bird magnet. I felt like the first kid in high school to
get a car—suddenly I had a lot of friends and visitors.

Then I noticed that with the increase in birds came a
decrease in bugs and pests in the garden. I would gaze out
the window and watch birds poking in and around the roses
for insects. *You little darlings,* I thought. *Go for it—stuff yourself on those evil aphids!* In the spring, after I had dug around
the plants and amended the soil, I could see robins pulling
up worms. I watched sparrows, wrens, and robins making
nests out of the clippings I left behind after pruning. In late
summer, the sunflowers may have been nodding off and
looking past their bloom, but the birds loved picking out the
seeds they produced. In the fall when I got behind in my
pruning and the rosebushes produced hips and the mountain
ash produced its red berries, they were all covered with hap-

pily munching birds. Even the dead tree in the backyard that I kept putting off getting removed was the happy hunting ground for woodpeckers in search of bugs. I discovered that my lackadaisical gardening style has an added benefit: it attracts birds.

This is truly a good thing for people who don't have the time or inclination to run around and make their place look like it's on the Parade of Homes tour. When every bush, plant, and tree is pruned and sprayed with pesticides to immaculate perfection, it discourages our feathered friends from visiting and making their home among us. I won't eat food doused with chemicals, and the birds won't either. I feel more comfortable in a friend's home when it's slightly cluttery than when it's pristinely presented, and so do the birds. They need our densely overgrown bushes to hide their nests in. We shouldn't be so quick to make nature bend to our wills with our power mowers, trimmers, and weed whackers. It's not difficult to attract birds to your place—just make them feel safe and give them something to eat and drink.

So what do they like to eat? Before you run to the store and grab a bag of birdseed, you might want to experiment with free food. The cheapest and smartest thing we can do to feed the birds is to grow native trees and shrubs. When I first began attracting birds that's all I had: berry-producing shrubs and water. I didn't put up a bird feeder because I knew seed on the ground would encourage the exploding skunk population we already had in our neighborhood. I attracted plenty of birds with my seed-producing plants, berry-producing shrubs, and water fountain. Besides, everyone else in the neighborhood was putting out the same seed from the same stores. I wanted to offer them something special and guaranteed to make them happy—the food that God first offered them.

In my old neighborhood in California, I noticed that the birds loved the mountain ash, holly, cotoneaster, crab apples, mulberry, and hawthorn trees and shrubs that grew locally. I've seen these same plants growing in many other parts of the U.S. as well. But for a more comprehensive list, there is a great book from Thunder Bay Press titled *The Audubon Backyard Birdwatcher: Birdfeeders and Bird Gardens*. It includes an *extensive* detailed list of evergreen trees, berry- and seed-producing trees, and plants that will grow well in specific regions of the country. There are separate lists for the northeast, southeast, prairies and plains, mountains and deserts, and Pacific coast regions. It also has illustrations of where to put plants in your bird-friendly garden. Along with the hundreds of fantastic color photographs of birds, plants, and feeders, it is a valuable resource for both the beginning and advanced birder who is interested in providing a friendly backyard haven for birds.

But maybe you're not the type who is content to let the garden go to seed while you put your feet up and sip iced tea. Maybe you're like my friend Mary Jo, who just can't get that Martha gene out of her system and wants to *do it right*. In fact, you want the prettiest and *best* backyard in the neighborhood, to encourage the *most* birds. Even better would be a plaque that shows your garden is certifiably superior. If that's you, the National Wildlife Federation has a wonderful plan for your life.

I had just discovered my local Wild Bird Center[1] store (and was happily buying up CDs on birdsong, suet feeders, and hummingbird feeders) when Bonnie, the congenial owner, found out I was writing a book on birds. "Here," she said, handing me a packet of information. "You'll be interested in this." Inside I found fascinating tips and advice on how to certify your backyard as a National Wildlife Federation Backyard Wildlife Habitat. The NWF is partnering with Wild Birds Unlimited stores and Home Depot to help more people join the 23,000 households that already have their backyards certified as habitats. It's a cinch to do. In fact, if you're an enthusiastic gardener and birder, you may already qualify. Craig Tufts, the chief naturalist and manager for the Backyard Wildlife Habitat program, described in his introductory letter how little space it takes and how rewarding it is for the family:

My own yard, habitat #2364, is less than a quarter acre. During the past eleven years, over 150 kinds of

---

[1] Wild Bird Center stores: *www.wildbirdcenter.com* or 800-WILDBIRD. For Wild Birds Unlimited stores: *www.wbu.com* or 800-326-4928. Both have great products and links.

shrubs, trees, and flowers have been planted, providing habitat for many feeding and nesting birds. More than forty-six kinds of butterflies have visited this habitat looking for nectar and places where their caterpillars might find a healthy food supply. As my sons grew up, they enjoyed going on critter safaris, discovering spiders and insects, such as dragonflies and water striders, surprising turtles and toads. . . . The yard remains a source of wonder and excitement for them.

To qualify your place as a habitat, just provide the four basic elements: food, water, cover, and places to raise young. The information packet shows you how to put your habitat together. It lists the plants that provide food and shelter and different ways to supply water. It includes the plants that you should avoid because they are invasive, and it also lists different kinds of birdhouses and seeds birds enjoy (a good starting point is *www.nwf.org/backyardwildlifehabitat/*). For more in-depth information the packet includes several Web sites, books, and organizations to contact. Once you qualify you will receive a personalized certificate and an assigned

number for your habitat from the NWF. After qualification you can also "purchase and post an attractive yard sign to educate friends and neighbors about your Backyard Wildlife Habitat project." As a gardener who's put in many hours of backbreaking, sweaty, and thankless labor, I like the idea of someone certifying my efforts and commending my attempts to go the extra mile. Too rarely do we get recognition for our tasks around the home. I'm an approval addict and am always eager to hear "Well done!" It's rewarding to make different varieties of God's creatures feel at home.

I wish more churches would attempt to do the same. I grew up in the Midwest suburbs, and to look around our congregation you would've thought it was the twinset-and-pearls church of blue hair. Everyone was from the same socioeconomic group; everyone was white and most were of an older generation. Which, in itself, isn't a *bad* thing; it just wasn't my thing. It didn't give me a vision for the wider church around the world. It made me feel like I was in a country club, not a church where the purpose was to worship God and reach out to ease the suffering around us. When I moved to California in the early eighties, I was shocked to see people attending church in blue jeans, cutoffs, and any old thing they threw on that day. Then I noticed that because there wasn't the expectation of suit and tie or skirt, a more diverse group of people showed up. There was also a time set aside during the Sunday night service where people could stand up and give praise reports on how God had met their needs that week or share prayer requests for needs to be met. It was exhilarating to witness God moving in the community and prayers being answered.

When I moved to Australia for three years, I found a congregation that was even more diverse. I attended a church with electric guitars, modern worship music, and people from Greece, Vietnam, the Pacific Islands, Eastern Europe, and all parts of the globe. I reveled in it. I would pretend I was in a worship service in heaven, surrounded by my brothers and sisters in faith and all worshiping the same one true God.

There's a woman who attends the same nondenominational Bible study I do. Most of the women who show up are middle class, and the discussion leaders are encouraged to dress conservatively. But Jade shows up wearing at least ten earrings in one of her ears. She has rings on her fingers and on her toes. Her nose is pierced. Her eyebrow is pierced. She is probably in her late forties to early fifties, but she has long, flaming red hair. She wears eclectic clothing in vibrant colors. When I first met her, I'm embarrassed to admit that I assumed she was new to the group or that she was probably new to the faith. But I found out she's been a believer for many years. She has, in fact, a passion for God that makes me ashamed of my lack of enthusiasm. I pigeonholed her because of her unconventional look and approach to life.

The same issue works in reverse. Because people sometimes associate the term *Christian* with those who are narrow-minded, gullible, happy to slash and burn the environment for the almighty dollar, and heartless toward the poor, I keep my spiritual views to myself until people get to know me. Then they are surprised. They are even more surprised when they meet my husband. Tom is impossible to pigeonhole. In the seventies he looked like and lived like a hippie in a big house with lots of people. He used to make his own soap and candles. He also took in the homeless and got a Ph.D. in physics (bachelor's, master's, and doctorate in *six* years). He still cares passionately about social justice, but now he wears a suit and tie. He's CEO of a software firm and attends a mainline denominational church. His intelligence and compassion baffle those who are quick to call evangelical Christians disparaging names.

It is tragic that the world's view of Christians has become so antagonistic. For centuries, *Christian* used to mean the people responsible for setting up halfway houses and hospitals like William Booth of The Salvation Army, visiting the imprisoned, founding our most prestigious universities, and looking after God's creation like St. Francis of Assisi. Now it's associated with angry, self-righteous people who don't care about the homeless, those dying of AIDS, or the environment. In fact, when I put together the proposal for this book, my agent made me *remove* the word *environmental*.

"Why should I remove the word *environmental*?" I asked her.

"Because," said Janet, "Christians associate that term with liberal, tree-hugging greenies, and it's a red-flag word to them."

I was sputtering with disbelief. "But we are told in Genesis to be good *stewards* of God's creation! Christians should be on the forefront of not polluting this world and protecting the environment. This is ridiculous!"

"I know," she said, "but your argument is not with me; I'm just telling you what you need to remove so there are no obstacles for publishers to take on your project." I bowed to the suggestion but I vowed to rise to the challenge to promote environmental education.

Fortunately, this attitude is on the wane and there are now more and more Christian organizations that see it as our God-given task to care for our environment—His creation. The Evangelical Environmental Network (EEN) is a unique ministry that networks with individuals and organizations, including World Vision, World Relief, InterVarsity, and the International Bible Society. EEN's publication, *Creation Care* magazine, provides biblically informed articles on how to protect your family against environmental threats and how to more fully praise the Creator for His marvelous works. Best of all, it's *free*! You can contact the EEN at een@creationcare.org or call 202-554-1955.

Montreat College in North Carolina has a whole center

devoted to getting Christians involved in protecting our environment. Called the Christian Environmental Studies Center, its mission is "supporting collaborative efforts  between Christian environmental organizations, academic programming, and the Christian community."[2] An example of one of their interests is the Floresta USA organization. They are dedicated to Third World economic development and environmental restoration. Floresta provides slash-and-burn farmers with loans, technical assistance, and product marketing services to set up small agroforestry businesses. By facilitating the switch from subsistence farming to agroforestry, Floresta is helping the rural poor while halting the deforestation created by traditional farming techniques. Floresta is currently working in the Dominican Republic, Haiti, and Mexico.

Besides the word *environment*, *diversity* seems to be another hot-button word. Diversity means that all living creatures — including bugs, birds, snakes, and small rodents — are needed to keep the cycle of life revolving in our world in a healthy continuum. If we douse our gardens with broad-spectrum chemicals to wipe out aphids or caterpillars, we negatively affect (or kill) the birds, butterflies, toads, and tortoises that feed on these plants. Always strive for an organic method first. Wiping out one creature negatively

[2]*http://cesc.montreat.edu.*

impacts the whole. The same is true in our communities of faith. Although we may feel more comfortable being around or worshiping with others who look like us and act like us, that's not a real reflection of God's creation. We need to try to worship with and get to know those different from ourselves, to serve others who are completely unlike us. Try this and you'll probably discover a new dimension of God's grace and creativity.

The other day I signed up to be a mentor for women who recently have been released from a minimum-security prison. They are living in a group-housing situation where it is hoped they will learn new ways to cope with the challenges and frustrations of life. Am I nervous about this? *Yes*. Do I know what I'm going to talk about yet? No. Do I have any experience with women in this situation? No. All I'm confident about is that God can use me despite how inexperienced I am. All I know is that "all have sinned and fall short of the glory of God" (Romans 3:23). Therefore, despite the diversity in our backgrounds, my new friends and I will be on equal footing. I will undoubtedly learn much from them, as I hope they do from me.

By making our lives and homes safe havens for the vulnerable birds and people that cross our paths, we are given the wondrous opportunity to witness God's diversity and artistic creativity up close. And that's an environment for grace and growth. Maybe you'll have a plaque on your plot in heaven that reads, "This soul provided a safe haven for those in need and looked after my environment." I *know* you'll have "Well done, good and faithful servant" whispered in your ear.